Love, Coco x

M H Dunbar

T

Copyright © 2024 M H Dunbar

The moral right of the author has been asserted.

Apart from any fair dealing for the purposes of research or private study, or criticism or review, as permitted under the Copyright, Designs and Patents Act 1988, this publication may only be reproduced, stored or transmitted, in any form or by any means, with the prior permission in writing of the publishers, or in the case of reprographic reproduction in accordance with the terms of licences issued by the Copyright Licensing Agency. Enquiries concerning reproduction outside those terms should be sent to the publishers.

This is a work of fiction. Names, characters, businesses, places, events and incidents are either the products of the author's imagination or used in a fictitious manner. Any resemblance to actual persons, living or dead, or actual events is purely coincidental.

Troubador Publishing Ltd
Unit E2 Airfield Business Park,
Harrison Road, Market Harborough,
Leicestershire. LE16 7UL
Tel: 0116 2792299
Email: books@troubador.co.uk
Web: www.troubador.co.uk

ISBN 978 1805144 014

British Library Cataloguing in Publication Data.
A catalogue record for this book is available from the British Library.

Printed and bound in Great Britain by 4edge Limited
Typeset in 11pt Minion Pro by Troubador Publishing Ltd, Leicester, UK

Introducing Coco

On 6th March 2022 on a farm in Fife, Scotland, a golden retriever puppy was born. Since leaving his family at the tender age of ten weeks to live with two housemates on the side of a Perthshire hill, he has written regularly to his best friend, Karen, who was present at his birth. He opens his heart to her about all of the things that are important to him – food, freedom, love and canine rights.

Through his emails and letters, we can share the first year in the life of this young dog. A dog who considers himself to be very fortunate – he has a high IQ, extraordinarily good looks and a strong social conscience. His housemates struggle to keep up with the standards he upholds. Modesty and humility? Well, perhaps he needs to work on those.

Welcome to the wonderful world of Coco!

While his housemates made some suggestions on how this book could be improved, they were largely met with an upward tilt of a cold, wet nose and a stubborn refusal to be influenced. Coco knows his own mind and is happy to add literary genius to his long list of talents. To that end, he regards what you are about to read as all his own work. Knowing their rightful place in the hierarchy (canine first, all other species second, of course), Coco's housemates simply smile indulgently and bow to his superior intellect. With one small caveat…

Although the following letters are based on fact, Coco has a fertile imagination and may have inadvertently embellished his stories. He calls it poetic licence. His housemates regard it as part of his irrepressible spirit.

Message from Coco to Karen

21st May 2022

Dear Karen,

I've arrived safely at my new home and am taking a moment out of my busy schedule to let you know how I'm getting on. I realise you and the other puppies will be missing me already.

The accommodation here is adequate and there is a plentiful supply of toys. However, my new housemates could have saved themselves the bother of buying a cage for me. They like to call it a 'den' – huh! I have no intention of going into it – after all, who do they think they're going to be sharing their house with? A criminal? I've let them know that I much prefer the rug in the sitting room.

You'll be pleased to hear that I'm already pulling my weight in terms of the household chores. The moment I got here I noticed that the garden was going to rack and ruin, with flowers popping up everywhere. So slovenly! Even pleasant housemates, it seems, can be a bit on the lazy side. But you know me, Karen. I'm not one to shy away from hard work. I immediately rolled up my sleeves (metaphorically, of course) and got down to it.

It was simply a case of biting the heads off those completely unnecessary flowers. Now, doesn't that sound much better? I wasn't done, though. Then I dug up all the moss between the flagstones. A most satisfactory morning's work.

"Well done, Coco," I hear you say. Indeed, I had hoped for recognition of all my efforts in the form of a few treats. Not a bit of it. Very mean-spirited, my new housemates. Nice enough people, but they need to work on their appreciation of a good job well done.

Nothing daunted, I have started a survey of all the ditches in the surrounding area, especially the muddy ones. As you know, this is something for which I have a special talent. It is no small task, but, again, seems to go largely unappreciated.

I've also taken on the responsibility for doing the shopping. Today, my housemates came, too (they like to tag along all the time). I particularly wanted to buy a harness and I found one in a very fetching shade of red, which shows off my golden fur to perfection. So much so, I almost didn't make it home! The ladies in the shop were very flirtatious and kept on saying they wanted me to stay with them. Shameless, but understandable – I did look devilishly handsome.

Karen, I'm not sure whether I should mention it, but… I must. It's troubling me so much. How can I put this to cause the least offence? Hmm… I wonder if you realise that my new housemates are, perhaps, a bit simple-minded – not the full shilling, if you get my meaning.

Maybe that's why you sent me to look after them. Yes, that must be it.

This is the problem in a nutshell: whenever I go to the bushes at the side of the house to do a pee, they follow me there and watch me intently. Then, once I've done it, they whoop with delight and shower me with treats. If I do a pee and a poo, they become positively ecstatic. I really don't think this lavatorial voyeurism is normal behaviour. Surely it is not unreasonable to expect a certain amount of privacy when one goes to the toilet. Anyway, I am resigned to the indignity on a purely temporary basis and resolved to expand their social and recreational habits.

Well, that's all I have to report for now. If I need rescuing, I'll send an SOS, but hopefully I'll have everything running just the way I want it in no time at all.

Love,

Coco x

Message from Coco to Karen

23rd May 2022

Dear Karen,

Life is ticking along here nicely, you'll be pleased to hear, with just the occasional example of inexplicable behaviour on the part of my housemates. Yesterday, I took one of them to Loch Tay. I understood that she wanted to go for a swim and that I would be there to guard her clothes while she was in the water. I was more than happy to oblige as it would allow me a good ten minutes of quality uninterrupted time to chew her shoelaces – a pleasure I indulge in a few times each day.

Imagine my horror, then, when I realised that we were going to the loch and she expected me to have a swim. No, no, no, no, no! Not this puppy, thank you very much. I prefer to have my four paws firmly planted on *terra firma* at all times. I'm simply not the floaty type – do people not realise this? There were some folks going past in an odd-looking boat – I believe my housemate called it a kayak, or some such strange human word – and they invited me to swim over to join them. I just pretended I hadn't heard.

As I appear to be something of a celebrity, I find it gets pretty tiresome being recognised all the time when I'm out and about. I guess it's something one simply has to get used to though and it is happening to me a lot.

'Oh, look, it's the Andrex puppy,' people coo. I'm perfectly happy to pose while they take out their pocket cameras and snap a photo, although I can't help puzzling over why they have conversations with said cameras – you humans do seem to be a bit of a confused species, Karen, if you don't mind me saying so. However, what I don't particularly like is having my image linked to something as basic as toilet paper.

Before you ask, I know Andrex is toilet paper as it's the brand my housemates use. And I know what toilet paper is because – well, let's just say one of them decided I needed an explanation in full when I suggested it could be used as a carpet for the hallway and ran all the way from the downstairs bathroom to the front door with one end of the roll in my mouth to demonstrate what I intended. So, rather than a – well, you know – an intimate tissue, I feel I'm more of a sports car and Rolex watch kind of a guy.

I've seen Rolex watches on advertisements – I don't know what they do, but they're very sparkly and one would look simply divine beside my bed. As for sports cars, the housemates enjoy watching something they call Formula 1 on the television. I thought it would be a science programme, but instead, it involves a number of flat cars (why so flat? Have they been squashed by a bigger car?) going round and round a bendy track at tremendous speed. What fun! And the drivers wear the coolest onesies, Karen. I wonder if I could persuade the people at Andrex to enter the F1 circuit. Maybe I'll drop them a note.

I apologise for forgetting my manners and not thanking you earlier for the basket of goodies you gave me as a going-away present. My lapse in decorum must have come about as a result of shock – for one awful moment I thought that the training pads included in the basket were a type of nappy that I would have to wear while being house-trained. I was aghast – imagine the humiliation! – but then realised that they were for less-advanced dogs who don't know to go outside to pee. Of course, I wouldn't need them. Not sure why you included them, Karen. I'll put it down to an honest mistake.

On the plus side, I particularly like the dental chew – fresh breath is so important, I feel, especially when one is interacting with the opposite sex. Actually, there hasn't been much opportunity for me to do that yet. I did have a lovely romp with a three-year-old Lab yesterday, but I'd prefer a girlfriend nearer my own age. I'm looking forward to plenty of romance in the future.

Well, that's all for now, my eyelids are drooping. Off for a snooze, only my fifth of the day.

Love,

Coco x

Letter to Chief Executive of Andrex

24th May 2022

Dear Andrex Chief Executive,

Please excuse this unsolicited letter, but I have a business proposition to put to you in which I'm sure you'll take a keen interest. As a golden retriever puppy, I am writing on behalf of my brethren everywhere. You may not be aware of the fact that we are a very special breed of dog – highly intelligent, exceptionally good-looking and with a sunny temperament. We have no need for toilet paper, either for business or pleasure, so I find it rather surprising that you chose us as the breed to advertise your product, luxurious though it may be.

In order to rectify this grievous mistake, I would like to suggest that you consider creating an Andrex Formula 1 team, with myself as the poster boy. This would give your product some badly needed cachet and would be an immediate winner. I would charge only a small fee (let's just call it a sausage allowance).

Ah, I can see it now: flash, low-slung cars, the roar of

the engines and of the crowds, the popping of champagne corks; a handsome golden retriever pup (my good self, of course) sporting a leather onesie and crash helmet. The public would love it – don't worry about fame going to my head, I am already a dog of some distinction. I can assure you I'm happy to travel the world – Monaco, Rio, Dubai. I really don't mind, as long as the food is good. I'd have so much to tell my housemates back home, who, frankly, never seem to go further than a walk along the river.

You must admit, it's a win-win, is it not? The image of golden retrievers would instantly acquire the glamour it so richly deserves and Andrex sales would rocket by being associated with F1. In addition, it would lift us both above the rather tawdry image conjured up by toilet paper.

I look forward to hearing from you by return.

Regards,

Coco Canine Esquire

PS Let me know if you need my measurements for the onesie. It's a bit tricky at the moment as I'm still growing, so perhaps a selection in various sizes would be wise.

Message from Coco to Karen

27th May 2022

Dear Karen,

There has been some dreadful misunderstanding. I'm sure I asked you to place me in a home where sausages would feature regularly on the menu, but the catering here is well below par. Since I arrived, I have seen neither hide nor hair of a sausage – not so much as a sizzle in a saucepan. The housemates are still giving me that biscuit stuff you suggested, but I was just a baby then and now I'm a dog of the world. It's high time I moved on to sausages.

    There's no use hanging around to see if my housemates will eventually improve the catering (my goodness, they're practically vegetarian), so I'm requesting you pay a visit to the game dealer near you in Fife to ask if they will send me a weekly supply of their finest venison sausages. Next time you're passing, please place my order and ask them to send my goods urgently via first-class post. In fact, see if they would send them by drone; that would expedite the process and avoid the danger of the postie being nobbled by my housemates and told not to deliver any sausage-shaped parcels.

Damn the expense, Karen! Speed is of the essence. The situation is critical.

I also have to report a very worrying development, to which we should alert my brothers and sisters. You would think that depriving me of the sausages to which I am so rightly entitled would be enough torment, but no – my housemates have bought one of those infernal books about how to train golden retrievers. They should be banned! I am not a performing seal; I am a free spirit and must have autonomy to go where the muse takes me; not be bound by ridiculous rules and regulations.

I had a quick look at the book while my housemates were out of the room and was shocked to find – on page 68, to give you a point of reference – a whole section devoted to *not* feeding a puppy scraps... I mean, tasty morsels from the table at mealtimes. This is outrageous! In the absence of sausages, scraps from the dining table are my only hope of getting anything scrummy to eat. Besides, what's the point of having big, doleful brown eyes if they can't be used to elicit one's heart's desire from one's housemates?

I strongly believe that to deny a puppy scraps is an infringement of our rights and as soon as I have finished this email to you, I'm going to be writing a pretty stiff letter to the Dogs Trust to detail, in no uncertain terms, how they must respond to this outrage. They need to be lobbying Parliament to get this cruel practice stopped.

Yes, I know all about the political system of the United Kingdom, Karen. I watch the news carefully every evening, listening out for the day our local MP brings to Mr Johnson's attention the appalling truth that puppies *do not yet have the vote*. I couldn't believe my eyes when I did an online search on Poodle (why you humans insist on calling it Google, I will never know) for my local polling station so that I would be prepared to cast my vote at the next election, only to find myself and my brethren denied this right.

Something must be done!

In the meantime, I have a plan. Next time my housemates' backs are turned, I'm going to get hold of the book, go to page sixty-eight, rip it out and tear it to shreds. Just to be on the safe side, I will then eat it – it can't taste any worse than the biscuit stuff. Fortunately, I don't think my housemates have reached page sixty-eight yet – they're rather slow readers.

That's all the news for now. Looking forward to the sausages arriving.

Love,

Coco x

Letter to the Dogs Trust

27th May 2022

Dear Defenders of the Canine Species,

Re: Rights for Puppies!

I am writing to you about a most appalling situation. It has come to my attention that a book (perhaps one of several) is in circulation, the topic of which is the training of golden retriever puppies. Being one such puppy myself, I take exception to the very existence of this book and hereby strongly request on behalf of my brethren everywhere that you lobby Parliament to have it banned. Make it clear to MPs that they cannot expect the puppy vote at the next general election if they continue to allow this abomination to exist. OK, I know that puppies don't have the vote at present but, mark my words, now I'm on the case it can only be a matter of time.

In addition, I demand legislation to be passed in the House that makes it illegal to deny puppies scraps from the table at mealtimes. I have been informed that this is a growing problem, therefore it needs to be nipped in the bud urgently. There should be severe penalties applied to anyone who lives with a puppy, but does not feed them scraps. I'm thinking of a fine initially, escalating to imprisonment for repeat offenders. The SSPCA could be contracted to make spot checks at puppies' homes to ensure that scraps feature regularly at mealtimes.

It grieves me that I have had to write this letter. Why has the Dogs Trust allowed the practice of not feeding tasty morsels to puppies to perpetuate? What do my brothers and sisters and I pay our subscriptions for, if not to have a strong lobby in place to protect our civil rights – life, liberty and the pursuit of happiness (which means sausages and scraps on a regular basis).

Yours indignantly,

Coco Canine Esquire

PS. While you are attending to this matter with the utmost urgency, I shall be launching a campaign to have the electoral vote extended to dogs and puppies of all breeds. Inclusivity, inclusivity, inclusivity, that's my motto. I expect to have your full backing in this endeavour.

Message from Coco to Karen

3rd June 2022

Dear Karen,

I just want to put your mind at rest and let you know that I have found a very nice vet to take care of any little medical issues that may arise in the future. Her name is Jan; she is young and pretty and thinks I am a marvellous physical specimen. At least, I think that's what she said. What else could she have said when it is so obviously true?

However, Karen, I wasn't sure about her at first, especially when she started to root around between my back legs. She then declared to all present (my housemates) that my testicles had not yet dropped and we would need to keep an eye on them. Believe me, I inspect that part of my anatomy several times every day and I will be the first to know when they drop; my genitalia do not need someone else to carry out an investigation.

Anyway, I forgave her that mild indiscretion when she lifted me off the examination table, pronounced me to be a fine fellow (which my housemates and I knew already, of course). She also called me a bit of a character (whatever did she mean by that?) and gave me some treats. I am looking forward to a long and happy relationship with Jan.

Speaking of relationships, I made a friend yesterday – she's an eleven-year-old girl who's a relative of my housemates. Her name is Charli and we met on the North Inch in Perth. I have to say that we clicked immediately and had great fun chasing each other around.

Charli has a hobby that she loves a lot – trampolining. She showed me a moving picture on her portable camera, and I was amazed – she can do the most amazing acrobatic forward somersaults and twirls. I've been thinking recently that I ought to take up a new hobby; chasing a ball around the garden is so passé. Perhaps Charli will teach me to trampoline. I'm a bit nervous about it, so I'll suggest that we start with her carrying me as she jumps up and down and does her moves. Then we can slowly progress to jumping up and down together while she holds my paw so that I don't shoot off in the wrong direction. I imagine I could get quite disorientated if I'm doing a backward flip in mid-air.

I've done some research on Poodle and there doesn't appear to be a mixed doubles event in trampolining competitions, so Charli and I could introduce it. She has a lovely sparkly blue leotard that she wears and I will source a good dog tailor and get one custom made, so that we are a team. We've got a play date coming up at the beach in a couple of weekends' time and I'll ask her then.

That dreadful training book must still be around the house somewhere because yesterday one of my housemates decided that I should be taught to walk on the lead. Ahem, excuse me! I would like to point out that I know perfectly well how to walk on a lead – just keep close to my housemate's left foot and don't tug or pull – but, as they seem determined to underestimate my intelligence so badly, I decided to have a bit of fun by pretending that I had no idea what to do.

As soon as the male housemate attached the lead to my collar, I started dancing around, chewing it, running around between his legs and then – this will make you laugh, Karen – lay on my back and refused to budge. This went on for ten minutes until he finally gave up and went back into the house. I could hear him telling the female housemate that there was no chance I would ever walk on the lead.

Hurray! At least they've given up on that barmy idea.

Wish me luck with the trampolining.

Love,

Coco x

Message from Coco to Karen

6th June 2022

Dear Karen,

I must apologise if my spelling is not up to my usual standard – I can barely see. There is something truly dreadful that I have to report – I'm afraid that I've let you and the other puppies down badly.

You see, I've been suffering from a touch of wind recently – perhaps as a result of the amount of rabbit poo that I've been eating in the garden. My housemates must have noticed because all of a sudden, they've started wearing masks over their mouths and noses. Although perhaps they don't know *exactly* who the culprit is; they keep blaming someone called Covid who is apparently spiking. Spiking? Do they mean Covid goes around jabbing sharp pointy things into people? That sounds painful.

Anyway, I digress. If they didn't know before that the flatulence problem is mine and mine alone, they certainly know now. Earlier today, I went with them to visit an elderly relative in a care home and we were in the communal lounge when I suffered a particularly vicious attack. I'm afraid that I just couldn't hold it in and let rip.

Oh, the reaction was immediate. You have to remember that those poor dears are already in a fragile state of health and most of the time they move very slowly indeed. Not this time, though. Some of them were clutching their throats, others had tears streaming down their cheeks and those with access to things called Zimmer frames got out of the room as fast as possible.

Karen, I know what you're thinking. Yes, I should have run round and opened all the windows and then administered CPR to the most severely affected, but I'm ashamed to say I simply turned tail and fled for home. As I did so, I could hear the ambulance sirens in the distance as the paramedics rushed to the scene.

So that is why I am now hiding in the cupboard under the stairs with just a single low-watt light bulb for illumination – a fugitive in my own home. I fear I shall have to go into exile, probably to France. I shall become the Scottish Pimpernel (they seek him here, they seek him there, etcetera, etcetera.). As I understand it, the French are much more forgiving of the occasional gaseous exchange due to all the garlic they eat. I shall slip away tonight under cover of darkness and hope to reach the coast by daylight.

But every cloud has a silver lining and I'm told that French poodles go crazy for a good-looking guy in a kilt.

Au revoir. Je t'embrasse de tout mon cœur,

Coco x

PS When you have a moment, Karen, please could you look up how to say in French, 'Hello, gorgeous, would you like to come back to my place in the Rue des Chiens? I've got sausages for tea.' And speaking of sausages, I am still awaiting my first delivery from the game dealer I asked you to contact on my behalf. You did do so, didn't you, Karen?

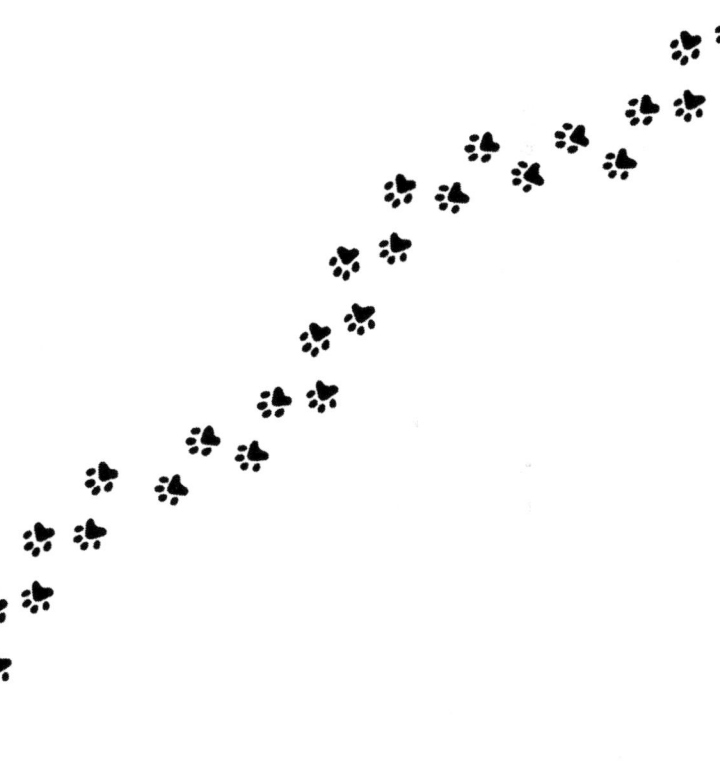

Message from Coco to Karen

8th June 2022

Dear Karen,

Please don't bother with that translation; I never made it to France. I thought that the Channel was just south of Perth and I had run out of supplies by the time I reached Edinburgh. So, I had to come back and hand myself into the authorities after all.

However, I'm pleased to report that I have been accepted back into the community, perhaps because no one actually died from the gaseous attack, although I believe a couple of the ladies are still on ventilators. So, at least I won't find myself behind bars, although I do have to fulfil three conditions. Firstly, I have to stop eating rabbit poo (such a shame – it's so tasty); secondly, I have to pay for the care home to be fumigated (where am I going to get that kind of money?); and thirdly, I have to write a letter of apology to the local community council. Overall, I think this is a small price to pay for my freedom.

Yours in *libertas*,

Coco x

PS I hope the good people at Andrex haven't heard about this unfortunate episode; it may make them question the advisability of hiring me.

Letter from Coco to the Community Council

8th June 2022

Dear Members,

As a responsible member of the local community, I wish to offer my sincere apologies for the unfortunate gaseous attack at the old people's home on Monday. I trust that everyone has recovered. As requested, I vow no longer to indulge in eating rabbit poo, which I hope to replace with some artisanal sausages that are due to arrive imminently.

I will also happily pay for the fumigation of the premises as I am expecting to come into a great deal of money shortly as the poster boy for the Andrex Formula 1 team. I have only one request of you: please do not leak this story to the media. My future career as a racing driver relies on my reputation being untarnished by puppyhood misdemeanours.

Humbly yours,

Citizen Coco

Message from Coco to Karen

12th June 2022

Dear Karen,

Now that everything is back to normal, I can bring you up to date with the rest of my news.

You may be surprised to learn that I've taken up yoga. Of course, I'm already physically perfect, but I thought it would help me chill out in a Zen sort of way. You see, I have manic attacks – usually about seven o'clock each evening, when I just have to career around the garden, frantically digging holes and stealing every sock or shoe that has been left unattended. I really don't know what comes over me and – understandably, I have to say – my housemates get a bit fed up. So, if I learn to chant and meditate, it may calm me down and I will stop being a hooligan hound for a period of time each day.

To this end, I joined my female housemate on the lawn to do some yoga. I was really good at the downward dog move and I managed the salute to the sun OK but what I was really looking forward to was the warrior pose. I thought it would mean baring my teeth and growling, but unfortunately it's more to do with pretending to fire a bow and arrow. I've really no need for human forms of defence, having needle-sharp teeth to deter any foe.

At that point I got a bit bored and distracted. My housemate's yoga mat is somewhat plain and ordinary looking, and could be improved by putting scalloped edges all around it, so I got to work with my teeth while she was in a deep meditation. But I was only part way down the first edge when she realised what I was doing and snatched the mat away from me. Such a shame as the squidgy feeling as I bit into it was most pleasing. For some reason, she was really annoyed. Lacking my entrepreneurial spirit, she clearly doesn't see the commercial opportunity that the introduction of scallop-edged yoga mats might present.

Anyway, she was so upset, I feel I need to apologise and give her a nice present to cheer her up. There's a dead thrush at the bottom of the garden – I've been saving it until it's rotted a bit more, but I'll present it to my female housemate now and I'm sure all will be forgiven.

Actually, I need to have a word with my housemates in order to get the house properly heated before the weather cools. We visited a friend last week and she has underfloor heating! It was lovely; I stretched out and fell fast asleep on it. I really think my housemates should get it installed. They speak of a time called the autumn when the weather starts to get colder and the nights draw in, whatever that means. How can a night draw? I mean, it's just a night, it has no hands to hold a pencil. Yes, I know I don't have hands either, but I don't pretend to be able to draw.

Anyway, if my housemates were to spend more time lying on the floor, rather than doing pointless stuff like yoga, they would be just as keen as me. After all, it can get fairly cold at any time of the year in our lovely part of the world; we don't have to wait until the night gets in touch with its artistic muse.

Lots of love,

Coco x

Message from Coco to Karen

16th June 2022

Dear Karen,

I'm astounded! The dead thrush didn't go down with my housemate any better than the tastefully scalloped edging on her yoga mat. I really can't understand why she reacted as she did and put my gorgeous present straight into the dustbin. So rude! Were I to be given a present – a kilo of sausages, for example (still no sign of my delivery, Karen, I'm getting concerned), I would be suitably appreciative.

However, harmonious relations have been restored, I'm pleased to say. So much so that we all went out for a run in the car today, up into the hills above Loch Tay. Not that the itinerary was all to my liking. I had just settled down for a snooze on a lovely soft blanket in the back of the car when my housemates decided we should all get out and have a walk.

Booooooooring!

That's just the kind of thing *they* like to do. Well, I dug my claws in, moved to the middle of the car where it was hardest for them to reach me and went totally dead weight on them. I held out for a while, but eventually, between the two of them, they managed to pick me up and deposit me in a most inelegant fashion on the grass verge. They may as well enjoy their little victory while they can. Given the rate I'm growing, they won't be able to manhandle me like that for much longer.

On a lighter note, I so enjoyed my play date at the beach with Charli at the weekend. We had great fun, although I had to steel myself to get my paws wet at the edge of the sea. I don't understand waves and how they keep coming, even when I bark at them to stop.

Stubborn waves aside, everything was going well. There were some other dogs to play with, so I was having a lovely time until a larger and more boisterous dog turned up. He was rather too rough for me and I got very, very frightened – so much so that I raced off down the beach. I was vaguely aware of my friends calling to me to come back, but I didn't. No chance, not with Mr Teeth-and-Claws strutting around like he owned the place.

Eventually, I stopped when I was at a safe distance from the rough dog. Charli came running to save me and we had a lovely cuddle, so then I felt brave enough to go back to the others with her.

I need to watch out for bigger dogs in the future. I thought they would be older and therefore wiser than me and would teach me the finer points of bottom sniffing and tail chasing, but now I know they're not all as friendly as they first appear.

Karen, do you know if there have been any other golden retriever puppies sent to this area? I ask, because when I'm in the sunroom at home, looking out through the floor-length windows at night, I see another golden retriever puppy in the garden each time. When I bark at him to go away, he just barks back at me in a very unfriendly fashion, as if *he* has a divine right to be in *my* garden.

I look for him when I go out into the garden but he must be very good at hiding because I never find him. Then, as soon as I go back into the sunroom, there he is again, looking in the window at me. My housemates are totally unconcerned about him and tell me not to be silly, that he's just called Reflection. Whatever sort of silly name is that? Furthermore, they say he's my reflection. You know how ridiculous that is, Karen; as if I would ever lay claim to owning another dog. And if I did, you can rest assured I would name him something solid and respectable like William or George, not Reflection.

But I don't mind admitting, I'm worried. What if there is a whole pack of Reflection's siblings in the garden? They may be trying to get into the house to steal my dinner. It would probably be best if I write to the SSPCA, just to alert them to the fact that there is at least one homeless puppy in the area, and there could be more. The SSPCA can take them away and find proper homes for them, rather than allowing them to terrorise innocent householders. I hope I will have more luck than I did with the Dogs Trust, who never did get back to me. Some people, Karen, are just so ignorant of basic good manners. Anyone would think that the Dogs Trust isn't equipped to deal with letters from dogs. Ridiculous!

Love,

Coco x

Letter from Coco to SSPCA

17th June 2022

Dear Sir/Madam,

I am writing to report a pack of golden retriever puppies that appears to be on the loose in Highland Perthshire. The puppies are clearly homeless, living in people's gardens and acting rather aggressively towards householders as they try to encroach on our territory. In my personal experience, they send a representative to stare in at windows and bark at the occupants inside. I live in fear of the one I've encountered coming into the house, eating my dinner and taking over my bed and toys.

Please would you be good enough to come and capture and rehome them? You will have no problem, I'm sure, as they are rather handsome creatures – much like myself, in fact – so people will be queuing to take them in. Although I have to warn you, they are slippery individuals. Whenever I leave the house to confront them, there is no sign of them, not even a vague scent on the breeze. It's like they cease to exist.

However, I'm sure you are well equipped to deal with situations such as this, so I will leave the matter in your capable hands. If it's any help, my housemates seem to know the one in our garden; say his name is Reflection. Meanwhile, I am double-locking the doors and windows at night and making sure that all my valuable toys are inside whenever I am not outside to guard them.

Yours in worried anticipation.

Coco Canine Esquire

PS I understand that you are a charity and, as such, may hand out essential daily needs to puppies in distress. If that is indeed the case, please send a kilo of sausages to me at the above address. I have tried to take action myself, but to no avail and I remain deprived of these necessities.

Message from Coco to Karen

22nd June 2022

Dear Karen,

As you are my best friend, I want you to be the first to know – I'm in love! The object of my affections is a gorgeous little cocker spaniel called Milly. She is just so cute and sweet that I have fallen completely head-over-heels.

What's even better – she has taken a fancy to me too. She's invited me to stay at her house in a place called Nairn for a weekend in July. I can't wait! We had such fun together running around the garden when we met for the first time at the weekend. Milly is four weeks younger than me, which I feel is ideal. As the more mature partner in the relationship, I will be able to help her with the daily challenges that all puppies experience: how to select the smelliest shoes to chew; where to find the muddiest ditches; how to recognise a soft touch for a biscuit treat.

I need to increase my spa treatments before going to Nairn, so that I will be looking my best. I can see us now, strolling paw in paw along the beach in the moonlight. Oh,

I mustn't get carried away, but I just can't help imagining how wonderful it will be to spend a whole weekend with my sweetheart.

Although there are aspects of my new home that I feel are substandard (mainly on the catering side – the sausages, Karen, where are they?), I must say it was very kind of you to fix me up with housemates who offer a daily spa treatment. I do so love a good pamper with a bristly brush and even with a slightly spikey one. Apart from the fact that it makes my coat look splendid and sorts out any tangles and dried mud, I just adore the massage that goes with it.

I always jump for joy when I see my housemate get the grooming brush out. I am told that not all puppies like it, but more fool them. I am happy to tolerate being brushed in rather sensitive places (behind my ears and, you know, down in that delicate place around my bottom) if it means a massage on the rest of my coat.

Karen, I wonder if you could help me with a small digestive query. I know, I know, I should consult with my housemates first, but I don't think they'd have a clue how to help. The problem is that when I am out for walks near our house, there is a particularly lovely, stagnant puddle that I like to drink from. However, the puddle is home to hundreds of little tadpoles and I think I may have inadvertently swallowed a few the last time I had a drink.

My question is: do tadpoles survive in a puppy's tummy, and if so, what will happen when they turn into frogs? I'm now frightened to yawn, which normally I do quite a lot, just in case one jumps out. Please advise urgently; I have a tickly feeling in my tummy and I fear the first of the frogs is getting ready to make a bid for freedom.

Ah, like a leaping frog, my mind has jumped back to Milly. Beautiful Milly. As she is my very first girlfriend, I want to make sure that I don't commit any faux pas. Please send me all the tips you can on conducting a successful romance with a cocker spaniel. People are much more relaxed these days about mixed marriages (am I looking too far ahead?), but even if we do attract some criticism, Milly and I will brave it out together. Love conquers all.

Will write again soon, but, in the meantime, don't forget to send me advice on the tadpoles. And the sausages. Actually, I may have the sausages covered, if the people at the SSPCA get back to me. Perhaps they are sourcing the finest gourmet links for me, but it's been a few days and no response, and Reflection is still in the garden.

Wait – what if Reflection is intercepting and eating my sausages? That's got to be it, Karen, because I know you wouldn't let me down. The outrage! The sheer arrogance of the creature! Will a puppy's woes never end?

If he tries to steal Milly, the fur will fly. This gallant canine will not forsake his love! Ah, Milly…

Your besotted friend,

Coco x

Message from Coco to Karen

29th June 2022

Dear Karen,

Oh no! My tricks on the lead have completely backfired on me. Yesterday evening, my housemates said that they were going to be attending an evening class – I thought it was just some boring old thing like learning to play the guitar or French conversation. They got ready to go out and I went to the door to wave them off when all of a sudden, they adopted a pincer movement, pounced on me, bundled me into the back of the car in a most unceremonious manner and set off at high speed, muttering that they were going to be late.

    I was hugely alarmed as I thought I was being kidnapped. I've seen reports on Poodle of puppies being captured by ruthless gangs and sold on the black market, and thought this was going to be my fate. Had my housemates secretly been heartless dog rustlers all along? Was that why they had deprived me of my right to daily sausages? Would I never see home or my darling Milly again? I barked and howled, trying to attract the attention of passers-by through the windows, but to no avail.

Anyway, we screeched to a halt after only a few minutes outside our local village hall, where a sign said 'Puppy Training Classes, starting 7pm Tuesday 28th June for five weeks'. Disaster! Well, perhaps not quite as bad as being kidnapped but, still, rather a blow to my self-esteem.

As it turned out, though, it was fine. There were only three other puppies signed up and they were all rather small and inexperienced. One of them peed as soon as he arrived in the hall and people had to rush around with a bucket and mop. What an embarrassment.

To help the other puppies along, the trainers used me as a role model to show them how to behave. It was pretty simple stuff, like recognising your name and touching your housemate's hand with your nose – things that I've been doing for ages. So, I came home with a tummy full of treats and my housemates were glowing with pride.

The only downside is that I have to go back again for the next four weeks because, without me there, how will the other puppies know what to do? Karen, it is my civic duty! They need all the help they can get – the lurcher seems seriously underweight, the dachshund's legs are about three inches long (he has no chance of finding a girlfriend) and the Shih Tzu's tail is growing out of her back instead of her bottom – she might need some corrective surgery. So I'll just have to do what I can to help them.

Many thanks for the tadpole advice. The tickly feeling has gone away. Such a relief. I don't think Milly would have been impressed to see baby frogs popping out every time I opened my mouth to tell her how lovely she is.

Being a dedicated follower of the fashion pages on Poodle, I know it is very trendy now to be vegetarian or even vegan. I hear people talking about pescatarian diets, flexitarian diets, gluten-free diets, lactose intolerance and all sorts of other stuff. Well, good for them, but I need to stress to my housemates that I am a red-blooded carnivore and I expect to get meat in my diet.

Recently, they've started to get concerned if I don't eat all of my biscuity stuff, so they occasionally mix in some cheese (vintage mature cheddar is my favourite), sweet potato or even banana. Can I just point out that while this may be tasty, it is not meat!

However, I've had an idea on how to make my housemates feed me better. As the highest authority in the land, the queen must surely be able to make them see sense and I know exactly who has her ear and can influence the situation.

Love,

Coco x

Letter from Coco to the Royal Corgis at Buckingham Palace, London

30th June 2022

Your Royal Highnesses,

In your highly privileged position, I expect you get many requests for assistance from puppies less fortunate than yourselves. I regret to say I am one of these puppies. You see, while you may have footmen and a personal chef to meet your every need, I have only some rather idle and dilatory housemates to rely on.

As a result, my diet is not sufficiently rich in meat and I would be most grateful to receive information on how much meat a royal corgi gets. I'm sure it's a lot and this could act as a model for my housemates to follow. If you have any particular recipes that your royal chef could share, that would also be much appreciated.

I am sure Her Majesty the Queen consults you on her annual speech to Parliament and on the passing of royal decrees, so a quiet word in her ear and you could be instrumental in improving the lot of puppies throughout her lands. Were legislation to be passed making it mandatory for all puppies to be fed quality meat at least once every day (in the definition of 'quality' I include sausages as well as steak pies, lamb chops and bacon), can you imagine the health benefits that would ensue and the much-reduced burden on veterinary services? Your loyal canine subjects would all be in peak condition.

Please share with me any information you have that might be useful for a parliamentary lobbying campaign which I am planning. If you would all like to come to Highland Perthshire to inspect this sad state of affairs for yourselves, you would be very welcome.

I look forward to hearing from Your Royal Highnesses.

Sincerely,

Coco Canine Esquire

PS I only have one single bed (although I may have to get a double bed in the near future if my romantic dreams come true) and two bowls, so if you do come to visit, please ask your footmen to include your own bowls and beds in the royal luggage.

Message from Coco to Karen

1st July 2022

Dear Karen,

I find myself in a rather delicate political situation and I thought to myself, *Who better to consult than Karen? She will be able to advise me what to do.*

As you know, I have been getting quite a lot of publicity recently for my 'Votes for Puppies' campaign and I've had an offer of help from a rather influential source, Dilyn at Number 10 Downing Street – the Prime Minister's housemate. Normally I would be delighted for my campaign to receive this type of attention, but you know as well as I do that the present incumbents of Number 10 have a reputation for alleged bad behaviour, riotous partying, lying and, in the case of Dilyn, having simulated sex with humans' legs. Even his housemates are rumoured to have complained about it.

What am I to do? I cannot risk the reputation of the Votes for Puppies campaign by having it linked to such a disreputable scoundrel, but nor can I create an enemy of someone who has a prominent public profile and the ear of the Prime Minister himself. I thought of drawing up a set of regulations with which Dilyn (and others) would have to comply, but, sadly, recent events suggest that the residents of Number 10 feel under no obligation to obey the laws of the land. Not even the ones they themselves passed!

Dilyn says that being a Jack Russell cross, he will bring inclusivity to the campaign and attract support from the terrier community. He seems determined to play a prominent role. I shall have to choose my words very carefully if I am to turn him down.

I currently have another conflicted situation, which may be temporary but is causing some problems with my housemates. You see, because I have grown large very quickly, people forget that I am only four months old and getting in and out of the car is still difficult for me. But I have become too heavy for my female housemate to lift and even the male one is beginning to struggle.

As a result, they have bought a set of retractable steps so that I can get in and out of the car without their assistance. But I don't like them. They're a bit wobbly. Someone needs to tell my housemates that putting a treat on each step of the retractable steps is not going to make me any keener to use them – especially as I can reach the treats without actually having to go up them. I'd much rather sit in the front passenger seat, which is easier to get into than the boot and means I could help with the navigation. I have looked up every butcher's shop in the area on Poodle Maps and could direct the housemate who's driving without hesitation to the choicest sausages around.

Karen, I will send you a draft of my letter to Dilyn and you can let me know what you think. I will need to be direct, but tactful.

Your protégé,

Coco x

PS I see on Poodle that Nicola has announced that there will be another referendum. I think I'd better check on her position regarding puppies – it's not clear from the SNP manifesto whether she is a supporter of Votes for Puppies or not.

Draft letter to Dilyn from Coco for Karen to check

2nd July 2022

Dear Dilyn,

How lovely to hear from you. Thank you very much for your offer of assistance for the Votes for Puppies campaign. As you know, it is a cause that is dear to my heart ~~and only the right sort of puppy should be part of the campaigning effort~~. As a ~~responsible~~ member of the canine community, you obviously appreciate how important it is that the franchise should be extended to puppies.

In your elevated position as a resident of Number 10 Downing Street, you're looked to by the canine nation for moral and political leadership and I think ~~you~~ we all need to ~~ask yourself~~ consider whether ~~your recent behaviour, and that of your housemates, is really in line with the ethics of our campaign. you~~ we can maintain the high standards that the campaign has set.

May I suggest that before taking on a prominent role with our campaign, you consider seeing a vet about getting some bromide or other medical aid to suppress your sexual urges. I offer this suggestion as a friend – one who is directing his own feelings ~~for the opposite sex~~ into a long-term, meaningful and monogamous relationship with another puppy. You may wish to think about doing the same.

Dilyn, I need to be straight with you and stop shilly-shallying around. It's my campaign; I decide who joins and I've closed the waiting list. So, you can't join. Besides, you might not be in Number 10 much longer, so enjoy it while you can and keep your paws off my campaign. I know you're only doing it for your own political ends.

Sincerely,

Coco

Message to Karen from Coco

3rd July 2022

Dear Karen,

You are so right and I agree that I didn't really get the correct tone in my draft letter to Dilyn. I just ran out of patience. I've taken your suggestions on board and a revised version will go out to him tomorrow.

Bad news! I'm going to have to give up on my hopes of becoming a trampolinist. I weighed myself a few days ago when I was sixteen weeks old and I was 20kg. Charli says that I'm too heavy for her to carry so we won't be able to do the mixed doubles routine as I suggested. I'm very disappointed, but I've got plenty on my hands with my various campaigns, which are really taking off.

People seem to think that us puppies have a wonderful life – an endless round of eat, sleep, play, poo. Indeed, I'm not complaining about any of those aspects, with the notable exception of the lack of meat in my diet, but sometimes I like to add a bit of spice to life by playing tricks on my housemates. They're very gullible and get taken in time and again. In case you think the other puppies could benefit from them, here are my five best tricks to play on housemates:

1. If meals are getting a bit boring, pretend that you're off your food and look doleful. This invariably results in them rummaging through the fridge and coming up with something tasty to add to your bowl. Personally, I favour vintage cheese, but if you're very lucky and live in a home where meat is eaten, you may get a few slices of finest beef.
2. Sometimes it's funny to see your housemates get exasperated and stomp around. A good way to make this happen is to go on a walk with them in the countryside, but wait until you get home and then have a poo on the front lawn. This always gets them moaning and muttering.
3. If you like to be groomed, as I do, but find the sessions a bit short, just wait until they think they've finished and then roll in a nice dusty place, preferably with some dried mud, and they will have to start all over again. It works every time!
4. I welcome all visitors to the house, but my housemates like to think that I act as a watch dog for them. So, now and then, preferably when it is dark outside, I sit to attention and look in a very alert manner out of the window. I may even growl a little just to add a touch of authenticity. They always jump to the conclusion that there are intruders trying to break in and they run around locking doors and windows. Of course, there is no one there but that stupid Reflection, who still

hasn't been picked up by the SSPCA (who also haven't delivered my sausages – what's a puppy to do?), but I like to keep them on their toes.
5. The older dogs tell me we are supposed to like going for walks, but to be honest, I can take them or leave them. However, I do like treats. So currently, I'm refusing to go for a walk unless I am enticed down the garden path by numerous treats. It compensates for the time spent mooching through the nearby wood, when I would be just as happy playing in the garden.

Off now to rewrite the letter to Dilyn.

Love,

Coco x

Letter to Downing Street

3rd July 2022

Dear Dilyn,

How lovely to hear from you and to know that we have your support for the Votes for Puppies campaign. This could be invaluable.

I have given careful consideration to the role you might play, bearing in mind your many other public duties and civic commitments. I appreciate that the time you can give may be limited and I want to make the best use of what you can offer.

My thoughts are that we should play to your strengths and ask you to head up a clandestine operation in the Palace of Westminster, where we are seeking to find out which MPs might be against Votes for Puppies. Not all MPs are making their views known. This will have to be done under conditions of great secrecy, so no public profile or announcements, but it will allow the campaign to target our limited resources at those MPs who may oppose us.

I expect you have your own black book of contacts that you can use to help you in carrying out this very important work, but, if not, I suggest you take a look at Boris and Carrie's address books next time they are both out. I'm led to believe they like to leave papers lying around, so you should have no trouble doing that.

Please keep me appraised of your progress as your undercover investigations move forward. I suggest that all correspondence between us should be marked 'highly confidential' and should be shared with no one else.

Dilyn, your contribution will be invaluable to the campaign. Although public recognition cannot be possible, I trust that our ultimate success will be reward enough.

Yours in confidence,

Coco

(Campaign Chief)

Letter from Coco to Nicola Sturgeon, Scottish National Party Leader

4th July 2022

Dear First Minister,

I am writing to you regarding your recent announcement about holding a referendum next October. While I applaud your wish to see Scotland become an independent nation once again, I am sorely disappointed to see nothing in your announcement about the puppy vote – which is surely critical to you securing a win in the referendum.

My housemates tell me that there are around nine million dogs living in Scotland. I can't actually count beyond twelve, but I do know that nine million is *a lot*. That means very many, you know, Ms Sturgeon – would you mind if I were to call you Nicola? Were you to introduce legislation before the referendum to extend the franchise to the canine population, you could add nine million votes to your tally – sufficient for a runaway 'Yes'.

I fear that your advisers have overlooked the key position held by the Votes for Puppies campaign. While we cannot instruct our members to vote Yes, the fact that Holyrood would be the first part of the United Kingdom to introduce the legislation would send your popularity ratings soaring.

As Chief of the Votes for Puppies campaign, I would be happy to advise you further on the necessary legislation and how to gain support for it among members of those households with at least one dog. The benefits would be immense. Holyrood would find huge support for such critical legislation as:

- Sausages on prescription from all butchers.
- Canine spa treatment on the NHS.
- Abolition of puppy training books and videos.
- Puppy representation on key advisory bodies, especially those related to canine health and welfare, adoption and rehoming.
- Development of a speed-dating app for lonely puppies.
- Mandatory teaching of puppy welfare in all schools.
- Longer jail sentences for anyone found guilty of cruelty to puppies (such as denying them scraps and treats).

Plus a multitude of other initiatives with which I could help.

Please feel free to contact me at your earliest convenience – together, we can boost your campaign beyond your wildest dreams.

Sincerely,

Coco Canine Esquire

(Votes for Puppies Campaign Chief)

Message from Coco to Karen

8th July 2022

Dear Karen,

This will be a quick message as the car is packed and we are off to Nairn in a few minutes, just as soon as my housemates have tested Covid. I still don't know who this spiky Covid character is and I don't really want to, so why they feel the need to test him or her is beyond me. Test Covid on what? The most handsome dog breeds? (golden retrievers, of course, with cocker spaniels – female ones – a close second.) The meat content of sausages? The life and times of Lassie? And what kind of silly name is Covid? It's as bad as Reflection.

    Karen, I am soooo excited at the prospect of seeing Milly again. I got my housemate to give me a particularly thorough grooming this morning and, though I say it myself, I am looking very handsome. I also had a good munch on the dental chews so my teeth are sparkly white and my breath is minty fresh. I took your advice and got a present for Milly – it's a squidgy chipmunk soft toy that squeaks when you squeeze it. She'll love it and every time she plays with it, she'll think of me. I will be in her thoughts and her heart even when I am back in Perthshire.

Oh, the housemates have put down those blasted retractable steps and are calling for me to get into the car. Must dash. Will write and tell you all about it when I get back from Nairn.

Love,

Coco x

Later That Same Day...

Dear Karen,

Oh, the heartbreak! The disappointment! I'm inconsolable.

I'm still in Perthshire because the Nairn trip has had to be cancelled and I won't get to see my darling Milly this weekend. This is all because stupid Covid failed that stupid test. Or my housemates are positive Covid would fail it. Or Covid positively failed it. Or… I don't know!

We were literally on the point of leaving – I had the back windows open so that the breeze would ruffle through my fur and keep me cool; I had made a very comfortable den with a couple of blankets; and I was looking forward to two hours' undisturbed daydreams about Milly. The world is a cruel place.

My housemates say that it may be a while before we can all go to Nairn, so I need to find a way of getting there under my own steam without incurring too much expense – I'm a bit short of the readies at the moment. The people at Andrex are being rather slow to come back to me on the sponsorship deal and I still owe the old people's home for the fumigation after my unfortunate flatulence episode. I thought I could make my own way to Nairn by rail, but it turns out that if I want a seat on the train, then I have to pay a full adult fare. Otherwise, I have to spend the entire journey on the floor! I can't turn up to see Milly all covered in dirt and dust off people's shoes, can I?

I've done some research on Poodle and discovered that human children can travel free up to five years of age, yet I'm only four months and will have to pay full fare! I'm absolutely outraged at this blatant discrimination against puppies and must do something about it. Someone with influence will need to help me, so I'm off to write to my MSP.

Yours, broken-hearted,

Coco x

Letter from Coco to John Swinney MSP

8th July 2022

Dear Mr Swinney,

Re: Free Rail Travel for Puppies

As a resident in your constituency, I wish to bring to your attention a most grievous case of discrimination against puppies. I am appalled that this practice still exists in a modern country such as Scotland, under the auspices of a government that professes to treat everyone with equal consideration, regardless of their status in life.

My complaint relates to public transport. As you may be aware, humans are allowed to travel free on trains up to the age of five, despite the fact they may sit on a seat. Puppies, on the other hand, can only travel free if they lie on the floor and get all dirty and dusty. Whatever happened to opportunity for all?

I wish you to understand that I am writing on behalf of puppies throughout Scotland, not just for myself. The current regulations could cause mental health problems and unimaginable social consequences.

Let us take a random example. Say a puppy who lives near Pitlochry, in your constituency, requires to travel to Nairn regularly to support a dear friend who might otherwise suffer from chronic loneliness and be in danger of social exclusion. If the Pitlochry puppy was unable to afford a ticket to sit in a seat and then he arrived in Nairn, after spending the entire journey on the dirty floor, he might look like a vagabond and his Nairn friend would be upset at his uncouth appearance. She might even refuse to acknowledge him and run away when he approached. The mental health and wellbeing of both puppies would be seriously compromised, in addition to which the Pitlochry puppy would have to travel all the way home again on the floor of the train and get doubly dirty and dusty.

This is merely an example, you understand. I really couldn't say for sure that such a case exists. I expect there are many deserving puppies who have chosen to remain silent, but who are suffering nonetheless.

Please do your utmost to redress this discrimination, so that puppies throughout Scotland may travel in style.

Yours faithfully (as all golden retrievers are),

Coco Canine Esquire

PS Do you know if they serve sausages on the Inverness line? I think it would be an excellent innovation if they did and I would be happy to advise on the most appropriate kind and do a test run for ScotRail. Please put in a word.

Message from Coco to Karen

11th July 2022

Dear Karen,

Shocking news from Nairn. I have a rival! It seems that while I was languishing here in Perthshire, distraught, Milly was entertaining another beau. His name is Rudi, he's a cockapoo and – this is the worst bit – he's nine years old. He can't seriously think he's a suitable suitor for a puppy who is young enough to be his granddaughter, can he?

Anyway, Milly came to her senses while he was there as I heard on the grapevine that he had to leave prematurely and was sent in disgrace to a relative's house. He was sent? No, Milly saw him off. I so admire her pluck and determination in saving herself for me. I shall write to her straightaway to congratulate her on her swift and decisive action, and so that she knows she is always in my thoughts.

Oh, Karen, you were so right to advise me to keep the collaboration with Dilyn a secret. You'll have seen that he and his housemates have been given their jotters (as we say in Scotland) and will be vacating Number 10 on 6th September. I must write to him immediately to let him know that I am dispensing with his services, as he will obviously now be something of a pariah in the corridors of Westminster and therefore no use in the Votes for Puppies campaign. I knew a rogue like Dilyn would be found out eventually.

Grateful though I am to you for arranging for me to be given a home quite far north in the British Isles, I am sorry to tell you that I am seriously considering emigrating… further north. This Scottish summer is far too hot for me and while my golden fur may keep me snug and warm when the nights get out their artists' pencils and start drawing in autumn, I feel baked alive at the moment. My thoughts are to head for Greenland or Lapland – both places where, I believe, the cold months are plenty and the summer temperature barely gets into double figures.

I'm hesitating, however, as I have to consider how I will make a living. You see, I've been giving some thought to future careers as I don't want to be a financial burden on my housemates or on the State and I've given up on my dream to be Andrex's poster puppy. Rest assured, I have kept a copy of my letter to the CEO, and if I find that he or she all of a sudden has 'a great idea' to move into Formula 1 with another puppy as the poster boy, I will take measures. Let me assure you, Karen, I will not let this lie.

However, this has left me somewhat financially embarrassed, and the only career path that I've been able to find for puppies in Greenland or Lapland is sledge-pulling. And that is an occupation generally reserved for huskies. While I may be able to use my equal opportunities platform to break into the profession, I'm not actually sure that I want to. I see my talents being more cerebral rather than physical and I'm not absolutely sure that I could keep up with the huskies. I'm more of a lolloper than a galloper. Also, they're a little too closely related to wolves for my liking and might turn on me if they regard me as an immigrant bent on stealing their jobs.

I wouldn't mind driving the sledge, but I don't think such a post is open to a golden retriever. So much for equal opportunities in the far north! Maybe I should stay in Scotland and make full use of the cool kitchen floor, stretching myself out so that every inch of my tummy is in contact with it during the hottest hours of the day.

Lots of love,

Coco x

Message from Coco to Dilyn, Downing Street, London

11th July 2022

Dear Dilyn,

I have been following events in Parliament very closely these last few days and I see that you will be vacating Number 10 at the beginning of September. While this comes as no surprise to me, I realise that you may be reeling from your change of fortune and not have given any thought to the implications for the Votes for Puppies campaign. As your networks within Westminster will now be in ruins, I propose that we part company on the campaign. I am sure that you will have lots of other things on your mind right now.

May I thank you for the limited assistance you were able to provide to the campaign while you were in post.

Yours aye,

Coco

(Campaign Chief)

PS If you find yourself homeless as a result of the political storms, please be advised that accommodation for itinerants can be found at Battersea Dogs Home, SW8.

Draft Letter from Coco to Milly for Karen's Comments

11th July 2022

My dearest, darling Milly,

I was so disappointed not to be able to visit at the weekend. Maybe you will consider me forward if I say that I had hoped we would get to know each other better and perhaps become romantically attached, but there, I've said it anyway.

Please don't take offence. It's because I think of you all the time and I would love to be able to call you my girlfriend. I hope you feel the same burning ardour for me as I feel for you and that we can resume our courtship just as soon as I can get to Nairn. As you will discover when you get to know me better, I am a highly committed activist currently lobbying my MSP to change the rail travel regulations so that puppies can travel free – on a seat – on the train. As soon as that is sorted, which I'm sure won't take long, I'll be up to visit you as quickly as possible.

Please don't go out with any other prospective boyfriends in the meantime. Wait for me, your true love.

Je t'adore,

Coco x

PS May I respectfully enquire about the sleeping arrangements for when I visit? Should I bring my own bed or will one be provided? I don't mind sharing.

Message from Coco to Karen

18th July 2022

Dear Karen,

The cheek! The outrage! As you know, I wrote to Dilyn making clear to him that there was no longer any role for him as a campaigner and he had the nerve to come back to me, practically blackmailing me if I don't allow him to stay on – in a paid position! According to him – and I know from my ongoing correspondence with Their Royal Highnesses the Corgis that there are fears about this in Buckingham Palace – far from being turfed out onto the streets as he deserves, he is going to receive a peerage and be elevated to the House of Lords. He says his housemate has promised to fix it and as they're 'good mates', he's sure it will happen. Furthermore – I can hardly bring myself to write these next words, Karen, but I must acquaint you with the horrible truth – he wants to represent Votes for Puppies in the Lords (for an undisclosed fee!) and has said that there could be difficulties ahead for the campaign if I don't go along with his plan.

I'm in a terrible bind – my principles won't allow me to give in to blackmail from this rogue, but, if he does get a peerage just imagine what damage he could do to the campaign. We may simply have to close down. Dear Karen, please tell me what you think I should do – you know I always value your advice.

On that note, thank you very much for your comments on my draft letter to Milly. Yes, I suppose it was a bit over the top, when indeed we barely know each other. I've toned it down, including taking out the bit about shared sleeping arrangements – even though it was only a cuddle I was hoping for.

In between my active correspondence and my campaign work, I manage to get out for regular walks. As you know, I am at heart more of a hearth rug dog than a great outdoors fanatic, but one has to keep oneself fit and in prime condition. There is just one downside to my fitness regime, though, and that is the number of ticks that invade my fur when I am on adventures in the undergrowth and forging through muddy ditches. Every time I come home, I have to ask my female housemate to find the ticks and pick them off me before they burrow into my skin. Fortunately, because my fur is golden and the ticks are black, it is fairly easy for her to see them.

I don't understand why something like a blood-sucking tick has evolved. What use is it to anyone?

Don't forget to send me your thoughts on what I should do about Dilyn. That rascal has already caused me several sleepless nights.

Love,

Coco x

PS If you have any tips on how to covertly disable a vacuum cleaner, please send these by return. I'm keen to get rid of this pesky machine. Apart from interrupting my mid-morning slumbers, it also sucks up some of the carefully selected leaves and twigs with which I have decorated my home. I need to rid myself of this added burden – and soon.

Message from Coco to Karen

20th July 2022

Dear Karen,

Another Tuesday, another puppy-training class. Yesterday evening, I demonstrated again how to do long-leash walking. It's pretty easy, but the trainer said I got a bit distracted – what a cheek! I just wanted to go over to chat with the lurcher. Nothing wrong with that, is there?

I'm sorry to report that the dachshund's legs have only grown about one millimetre – a barely discernible improvement. Maybe he could be sent for physiotherapy or put into braces to lengthen them. The Shih Tzu has stopped coming – she's probably recuperating from the corrective tail surgery.

Given this unbearably hot weather, I've been spending more time at home in the house and garden. I love the garden – especially at the back where it is quite steep. I do play-wrestling with one of my housemates and sometimes one or both of us slides down the grass – as I'm sure you know, our garden is on a hill – and can't stop. It's great fun.

My favourite game is sneaking up on my female housemate from behind, pushing with all my weight and then somersaulting on top of her. She doesn't seem to mind and just laughs with me when we tumble down the slope together. Also, there are lots of apple trees in the back garden and I do like crunching on the windfalls.

If there are sheep or cows in the field beyond, I watch them carefully. The cows, in particular, are a lot bigger than I am so I'll just keep out of their way. The field on the other side has two ponies in it. Although one of them, called Mick, is a bit aloof, the other one, a little Shetland pony, and I are already good friends. He is called – you'll never guess – Coco! What a coincidence.

I go over to have a mooch around with the equine Coco whenever I get a chance. When I feel the time is right and we have become close enough that he won't take offence, I may suggest that he goes to WeightWatchers for ponies. He's really very tubby and because his legs are quite short, I'm worried that if he ever rolls over on his back, he may never be able to get up again.

Now that I can manage stairs better, I have taken the opportunity to check out what is on the upper level of the house. Well, what a swizz – my housemates never told me that there are three lovely big comfortable beds up there, any one of which I'd be happy to call mine. But I'm not allowed up at night – my housemates put a barrier at the bottom of the stairs and I am stuck in the kitchen with my puppy bed.

Actually, that's getting a bit small for me as I've grown so much. Maybe I'll be allowed one of the upstairs beds soon.

Love,

Coco x

PS Thank you so much for your suggestion on how to put a spoke in Dilyn's wheel. Just off to sort that out now.

Message from Coco to the Royal Corgis, Buckingham Palace, London

20th July 2022

Your Royal Highnesses,

Please forgive me for asking for your help once more, but I fear the issue we have been discussing recently – the rumours that the outgoing Prime Minister is planning to use his privilege to nominate his friends and cronies for peerages, including that rogue Dilyn – is one with which only you can help. I don't believe I exaggerate when I say that this possibility jeopardises the very status of the monarchy!

Allow me to elaborate. Apart from blatant nepotism, it is an affront to Her Majesty to suggest that she might have to knight a puppy so clearly unworthy of a gong. Please do whatever you can to sabotage this proposal and tip off Her Majesty that her position is being degraded and her good nature exploited by this disgraceful cronyism.

Yours in high dudgeon,

Coco Canine Esquire

PS Thank you for all your efforts to ensure the inclusion of meat in puppies' meals. I notice that I am now starting to get some pieces of ham and chicken mixed in with the biscuity stuff, so you are having an impact. Please keep up the good work with Her Majesty, so I that I can look forward to a juicy steak one day.

Message from Coco to Karen

27th July 2022

Dear Karen,

Thank you so much for your invitation to the party next March. I realise it's seven months away, but I'm already super-excited. Imagine twelve beautiful golden retriever puppies getting together for our first birthday party. It will be amazing.

My housemates have asked if they can come along, too, so I've agreed. I hope that's OK. It will also be lovely to see my mummy and daddy again, as well as all my brothers and sisters (and half-brothers and half-sisters). Will I recognise who is who?

I'm pleased to report that the puppy training classes have finally finished – what a relief. The lurcher has picked up a thing or two, but as for the dachshund… well, your guess is as good as mine. As it was the final session last night, I decided I would tease my housemates a bit. After all it was their dreadful idea that we attended in the first place.

When the trainer asked if there was anything the gathered housemates were having problems with, mine mentioned that I was reluctant to use the steps to get in and out of the car. The trainer said that she would try. She held a treat in front of me and I positively skipped up and down the steps – three times!

As we were leaving, my housemates tried to do as the trainer had done, but I refused to co-operate. I just sat at the bottom of the steps, looking at them balefully. It was hilarious, Karen, you could practically see the smoke coming out of their ears as they had to pick me up to get me in.

Since then I've been practising coming out of the car by jumping down and ignoring the steps, but I'm still not going in on my own. It's too hot in there at the moment and I don't know how long the journey's going to be – five minutes to the start of a walk or thirty minutes to Pitlochry.

Well, not only was it the last puppy training, it was also off to the vet again yesterday for another testicle examination. Jan says she can't find them and she'll have to look again at the beginning of September. I don't mind; I seem to be managing fine without them. Actually, I rather enjoyed the examination because while Jan was groping around between my back legs, the veterinary nurse gave me the most lovely cuddle and told me I was wonderful. It was a most satisfactory visit from my point of view, but my housemates seemed a bit anxious.

But, Karen, I've saved the best news for last… Milly is coming to visit on Friday. Oh, I can't wait! She said that if it was difficult for me to get to Nairn, then she would hitch a ride with her housemates and come to me. She is so resourceful and intrepid. I'm preparing a lovely lunch for her and I've dusted off the squidgy chipmunk present that I bought for our aborted visit (I've only chewed it a little bit, occasionally, to make sure it works, you understand). So, with some extra grooming, we're all set. I do hope my housemates behave and leave Milly and me in peace to play together. I'll let you know how it goes!

Lots of love,

Coco x

Message from Coco to Karen

30th July 2022

Oh, Karen, I'm exhausted. Completely cream-crackered, as they say in the Cockney vernacular. I can barely raise a paw to send you this message.

Did I mention that Milly is a cocker spaniel puppy? I hope to write properly tomorrow when my body should have recovered. For now, I must just lie in a cool, dark place and sleep.

Yours *defatigatus*,

Coco x

Message from Coco to Karen

31st July 2022

Dear Karen,

I feel strong enough now to write you a proper message, though it may be a few days until I am fully fit after Milly's visit. You see, I had thought that she and I would play together a bit, maybe lie down and have a cuddle and then play again a little bit later. I really had no idea what cocker spaniels are like – she just wanted to play and play and play. I tried to keep up with her, but golden retrievers aren't really built for speed and agility and we take our exercise in short chunks.

When I got too tired, I lay on my back, but then she came and tried to coax me to play. She even nipped my cheek at one point. Karen, is that what you call a love bite? If so, I can't say I liked it very much. And then, when I did play with her, I ran too fast at her, and bowled her over as she is still so petite and she yelped. Then I felt awful in case I had hurt her.

Oh, oh, oh – I'm not sure what to do because I fear we

may not be compatible after all. Anyway, she says that she regards me as a big brother, so I don't think she sees me in a romantic light. Maybe that is for the best. Still, we did get on well, so I haven't given up hope entirely.

My housemates behaved impeccably and they have promised to take me up north in the middle of September to see Milly again. Hopefully, finally, I will get to Nairn. In order that I don't get so exhausted, I've asked my housemates to get in a supply of energy drinks. I'm going to start a daily programme of calisthenics and on the morning of the trip I'll have a double-shot espresso coffee. That should all stand me in good stead for another Milly whirlwind.

Going back to bed now. Will write again soon.

Love,

Coco x

Message from Coco to Karen

1st August 2022

Dear Karen,

Perhaps you've been wondering what a typical day is like for me, here in Perthshire. Well, I hardly have a moment to myself, I'm so busy. I generally wake up about 5am and have a look out of the window. If it's too sunny, I go back to bed. If it's too dull, I go back to bed. If it's raining, I go back to bed. I then enjoy a couple of hours of light dozing and give some thought to all the duties I have to perform in the day to come.

Around 7.15am, one of my housemates will come downstairs to let me out. While I attend to the call of nature, they will fix my breakfast. I enjoy my breakfast a lot, although I do often get the hiccups after it – it has been suggested by the housemates that I eat it a little too quickly. They are always running their fingers across my ribcage to check that I'm not putting on too much weight.

Huh! Fat chance. Get it, Karen? *Fat* chance? Anyway, I'm a growing lad and all these calories are going to make me bigger and taller. People I meet can't believe I'm not even five months old yet.

After breakfast, now I can climb the stairs, I help my female housemate choose what to wear for the day and check that she's got her shoes on the right feet and has done up her laces properly. I'll often have a short kip while she's getting ready as the carpet on the bedroom floor is rather comfortable.

However… oh, Karen, this is a big however. A huge however. I have a bone to pick with you. A metaphorical bone, you understand, not a real one.

There is a funny sort of window in the bedroom, which looks on to another bedroom exactly the same, only in reverse. Furthermore, who should I see in said bedroom but Reflection? Oh no, I thought, he's got into the house! I was mortified.

But… Karen, you've been laughing at me, haven't you. As you well know, I'm a resourceful pup, so I decided to take the fight to Reflection; I'm top dog in this house and, handsome though he undoubtedly is (unsurprisingly, but I'm coming to that), I wasn't about to let him take my place. Know thine enemy! So, I put 'Reflection' into a Poodle search, and can you guess what came up?

Can you?

You can, can't you. Reflection is an image of me, only in reverse. Did I mention how handsome he… I mean, I am? I knew it! But, Karen, you allowed me to be misled. Effectively, I reported *myself* to the SSPCA as a stray pup. I've been so cross with them for not getting back to me, but now I must say, I'm rather relieved they didn't. Not sure how I'd have wriggled out of that one.

Anyway, you can understand why I needed to get that off my chest. I'll forgive you this time, Karen, but no more misleading me. Agreed?

So, back to my busy daily schedule. Once we're back downstairs and my housemates are having their breakfast, sleep often overcomes me again. I give into it as I know what's coming – a walk up the hill! This can be rather more strenuous than I like, so I need to conserve all my strength for it.

However, the walk can also be fun. We might see deer or rabbits and there are usually a few birds to chase. When we get home again, this is when I work on my various campaigns. As you can imagine, it's quite taxing juggling all the balls in the air – Votes for Puppies, Free Transport for Puppies, Daily Sausages for Puppies etc.

There is also my new venture – setting up Online Dating for Puppies, which is going to be very time-consuming. I'm just at the stage of drafting the profile questionnaire which I thought I would trial on Milly and myself before rolling it out to the general canine population. I need to put in all sorts of safeguards to stop villains and rogues getting on to it. Dilyn need not apply!

Around 11.30am, I stop for lunch, which I enjoy a lot, despite it bringing on another bout of hiccups and usually a big burp. Exhausted by my morning efforts I then need to have another sleep – generally spread across the kitchen floor so that my housemates know I am always available should there be any leftovers needing to be consumed.

Around 2pm, one of my housemates will come with me up the back garden for playtime. I burrow around in the bushes, eat the sheep's wool that's attached to the fence and terrorise a few plastic flowerpots that I have stored up there. Then the housemate and I do some play-wrestling and eventually we come back down to the house. If my blankets and towels are on the washing line, we'll gather them in on the way.

Then, I'm pleased to say, I enjoy one of my highlights of each day – being groomed. Ooooh, I do love it. At 3.30pm, it's time for my next meal, for which I am more than ready, having used up so much energy.

As you can well imagine, I'm in need of another sleep after that. If it's not too hot, I might have this on the front lawn. Late afternoon, I deal with personal correspondence – I get so many letters from other puppies who have heard about me, asking for advice on a whole range of topics. Some of them – it's so very sad, Karen – are from puppies with thoughtless housemates who don't understand their emotional and physical needs. I enclose one I got recently along with my draft reply. Please let me know if you think I've got the tone right.

Early evening, it's time for dinner, which I hugely enjoy and like to savour as I know it will be my last meal of the day. However, after I've eaten, my housemates generally ask me if we can go for another walk and I don't have the heart to say no. We might go to visit Coco the Shetland pony or hop in the car and go off to Loch Tay. Then it's back home for a snooze in front of the television before a last toilet stop. I need my sleep, Karen, so I make sure I'm in bed by 11pm for my much-needed solid six hours before my hectic schedule all starts again.

Whew! You must be worn out just reading this.

Love,

Coco x

Letter from Tiny to Coco

26th July 2022

Dear Coco,

I hope you don't mind me writing to you for advice, but I am at my wits' end and I have no one else to turn to. I am a chihuahua and my given name is Tiny. However, I prefer to go by the name of Titan.

You see, ever since I can remember, I have believed that I am in fact a Great Dane. I keep waiting to grow bigger, expecting to become imposing and to have other dogs – and people – respect me. But each time I look in the mirror, all I see is this skinny little dog.

Yes, people 'ooh' and 'aah' over me, saying how cute I am. I don't want to be cute – I want to be regal and to have other dogs run away when they see me coming. When I bark, I try to make it as deep and growly as possible, but all that comes out is a high-pitched yappy sound.

That's not who I am – in my heart, I am a fearless leader, in front of whom all other dogs tremble. What can I do? I don't want to live the rest of my life not being taken seriously and carried around in a basket with people laughing at me.

Oh, Coco, you are so wise and you seem to have your life very well organised. Please tell me what to do.

In despair,

Tiny (aka Titan)

Draft Reply from Coco to Tiny

31st July 2022

Dear Titan (for that is what I shall call you),

I'm very happy that you have contacted me, as I hate to think of you suffering alone. First, let me explain that the condition you are experiencing is called 'breed dysphoria'. You may wish to read all about it on Poodle, as I did.

It is not uncommon in a mild form, but you seem to be debilitated by a particularly severe case of it. Usually, it occurs in large breeds, especially one which is renowned for its bravery, where certain individuals may in their hearts be timid and run away from any loud noise (such as fireworks) or unexpected movement. It would seem your affliction is the opposite of the more common form, for your courage and leadership are hugely disproportionate to your small stature.

While there is no known cure for breed dysphoria, there are ways of changing your perception of who you are, so that it is less damaging to your mental health. Titan, let us consider whether it is necessary for your peace of mind to be looked up to by all dogs. Perhaps you need to work on managing your expectations and restrict your ambitions to smaller breeds only. Might it suffice to be looked up to by your fellow chihuahuas along with Toy poodles, papillons, mini schnauzers and a host of others? With your courage and determination, you could, I am sure, become a leader among them, setting an example for smaller breeds on living with dignity and how they fulfil an important function in the canine world. Courage and status are not the preserve of the larger breeds and certainly you don't need to be a Great Dane to have them.

Apart from suggesting that you work on your bodybuilding and bark-lowering, may I also advise on two other courses of action. Firstly, if anyone dares to laugh or coo at you, give them a good nip and then look angelic. I assure you they won't do it twice; nor will they complain to your housemates, who simply won't believe it of such a heavenly being. Secondly, consider using your sharp teeth to take apart the basket that you're carried around in. If that fails, just pee all over it. Your housemates will soon get the message and won't put you in it again.

Good luck, dear Titan. I look forward to hearing about your exploits as a leader among the smaller breeds. I am sure you have many adventures and triumphs ahead of you.

In admiration,

Coco

Message from Coco to Karen

3rd August 2022

Dear Karen,

Forget what I said about a typical day – everything has changed. There has been a complete turnabout and I'm feeling a bit discombobulated.

I had been thinking it was rather strange that my housemates were emptying out the kitchen cupboards and clearing the sunroom (they're not generally that conscientious about housework). Now, it turns out it was all to do with us moving to Edinburgh for a month while builders work on the house in Perthshire. What a shock!

So, I'm here in the city and I can tell you it is all very different from home, and from when I lived with you on the farm. There are so many new smells and the pavements are harder on my paws than the forest tracks. I don't want to look like a country bumpkin in front of the canine city slickers, so I'm quickly learning the ropes.

All the puppies here wear very smart collars or harnesses with their name tags on. So being as I am now the fashionable dog about town, I too have a new harness and a name tag – mine looks like a medallion and I feel quite the Adonis with it displayed on my handsome chest.

We don't go for walks in the woods anymore or along the riverside. Instead, we go to parks, which are like large gardens, and there we meet lots and lots of other dogs. My head is in a complete spin with the number of new friends I'm making. We go wild when chasing each other around, but I have to be careful as I don't think my housemates are used to the big city. They are certainly finding it harder to adjust then me; they're inclined to wander off, chatting to people they meet. One minute they're there and the next they've disappeared. It can be difficult keeping track of them and, dopey though they undoubtedly are, I wouldn't want to lose them. For this reason I keep them on a lead more often than at home.

One of the things I'm learning is that it's not actually rude to walk past someone without stopping to chat. When we're in the countryside, we see so few people and dogs on our walks that when we do we always stop to chew the fat (metaphorically, not literally, sadly) and have a play with the dog. Usually we know who they are anyway.

In the city, I started off doing the same, but there are so many people and dogs to greet that we never managed to get anywhere. I still try to be polite to everyone, but I think I need to be more discriminating about those I actually play with. Today, I had a lovely time with two Labradoodles, a Bernese Oberlander and several spaniels.

The other thing I like about the city is the café culture. I could become something of a flâneur – just sauntering from establishment to establishment observing society.

Yesterday, the housemates and I found a particularly good café. The waitress brought me my own freshly prepared bowl of water (I don't like sharing) and a large, delicious dog biscuit. In fact, I noticed on the way out that they had a whole jar of them on the counter. I'll be going back there again very soon.

So, I'm rather torn – I'm enjoying being in the city, but I do yearn for home in Perthshire. I'm really a country boy at heart.

Lots of love,

Coco x

Message from Coco to Karen

5th August 2022

Dear Karen,

Thank you very much for your comments on the letter to Titan. I'm glad you felt that I was sensitive but realistic. I'll let you know if I hear more about how he's getting on.

In the meantime, I'm wondering if you have heard any rumours about me receiving an award from the queen, perhaps in the New Year's Honours List. It's just that I think my housemates must have got wind of something, as they now occasionally refer to me as Coco CBE. Well, actually, they say 'CBA', but, as I've pointed out before, they're not overly endowed in the brain department, and it's an easy mistake to make.

Karen, it's so exciting! All my campaigning must have come to the attention of Her Majesty and so she would like me to have formal recognition for my efforts. I find my housemates usually let slip about my forthcoming honour when they are trying to entice me out for a walk and I am in the middle of a lovely daydream about my budding romance with Milly.

'Come along, Coco CBA,' they say as though showing me the respect I deserve (finally) will make me keener to go out. I generally just ignore them but it would be good to get some advance notice of going to Buckingham Palace to receive a CBE. I shall need a morning suit tailor-made; it's unlikely there will be any off-the-peg ones to fit me. 'Coco, Commander of the British Empire' has a very distinguished ring about it. Milly will be so proud of me.

I do hope that by the time I go to Buckingham Palace, I will have finished teething. My baby teeth are dropping out at a rate and I'm a bit gummy at the moment. I wouldn't like Her Majesty to think that she is giving an award to a puppy who requires false teeth and forgot to put them in that morning.

In other news: another day, another café. Today's one only had a shared water bowl for dogs and no treats. I've scored it off the list of dog-friendly cafés I'm compiling, with a view to publishing a guide – a bit like 'Scotland The Best' only from a puppy's point of view. It should be a winner!

Lots of love,

Coco x

PS I would really appreciate some careers advice from you, Karen. Here in the city, I see everyone rushing off to work each morning and going home tired at the end of the day and I must play my part. I'll give it some thought and come up with a few ideas to run past you. I hope that's OK.

Message from Coco to Karen

11th August 2022

Dear Karen,

I am really not enjoying this heatwave – especially here in the city where the heat seems to radiate off the buildings. Thankfully the housemates and I are only going out early in the morning or in the evening when it is cooler. I get so hot running around, even for a little while, so it spoils my playtime with other puppies in the park. Some of them tell me they have had their coats clipped for the summer so they will be cooler, but I'm not sure I would like that – I don't think I would suit a short back and sides, do you?

Each day, my housemates and I listen to the weather forecast so we can plan our walks and playtime. From a golden retriever's perspective, I have to say that I find the weather reports very misleading. They are far too human-centric.

Let me give you an example. The forecaster might say, 'It will be pleasantly warm today', which is fine if you are a human and can wear a vest and shorts. But if you wear your winter coat all year round, then 'pleasantly warm' actually means 'boiling hot'. I shall have to pick up my pen and write to the Met Office (I did a bit of research on Poodle to find out who is responsible for predicting the weather). I'll get them to be more inclusive in their forecasting, and perhaps suggest that they could reflect this in a change of name to the Pet Office.

But despite the heat, I am actually in very good spirits because – hallelujah! – the corgis' royal campaign is really starting to bear fruit – or should I say bear meat. I had sausages twice yesterday and I can see that there are more in the fridge. Oh, Karen, they were delicious. I polished off the lot in double-quick time. Paws crossed for the rest tomorrow.

There is some kind of festival that has started here in Edinburgh. Everyone's talking about it, but I haven't seen any shows advertised that would appeal to a pup, so I don't think I'll bother. I'm hoping instead to go to the cinema, one that is screening *101 Dalmatians*. Although it's very scary in parts, it is my favourite film of all time.

Because I am still growing quite fast, my housemates sometimes call me 'Clifford', after *Clifford The Big Red Dog*. I'd quite like to see that film too as I've been told it has a happy ending – I'm rather sensitive and don't want to dissolve into uncontrollable sobbing in the cinema; that would be embarrassing.

We hear fireworks every evening. My housemates say they're from the Tattoo, but I don't understand. Isn't a tattoo something that you humans paint on your skin? Do you generally acquire one to the accompaniment of fireworks? What with the nights drawing in (drawing in where? No one has yet told me) and noisy celebrations of arm paintings, I fear humans are a little obsessed with pictures. At first, I was slightly alarmed by the fireworks every time someone gets a tattoo, but now I don't even bother to stir.

Love

Coco x

Letter from Coco to the Met Office

12th August 2022

Dear Sir/Madam,

I am not writing to you to be critical of the excellent service you provide, so I hope you will accept my proposal in the spirit in which it is intended. As a concerned member of the canine community I simply want to help you to improve your service further by making it more inclusive.

You will appreciate that for those members of my community who sport thick coats all year round, the way the meteorological data is translated into forecasts and advice for humans may be somewhat misleading. In order to prevent dehydration and heat exhaustion among the furrier breeds – such as Newfoundlands, chow chows, Pyrenean mountain dogs and, of course, golden retrievers – it is essential that you deliver a forecast appropriate to our particular situation.

My advice, if I may be so bold, is to have a gauge against which dogs can interpret the weather forecast. I see this as being on a scale of one to seven, which could be announced by weather forecasters on all the main media outlets. This table outlines the criteria for each number on the scale:

Level	Type of weather	Behaviour to be adopted
1	Below zero, snow and ice.	Get out into the garden as fast as possible and roll around on your back in the snow. Wriggle about so that the cool ice gets right through your fur, then give yourself a good shake. Repeat as often as you like.
2	Temperature around zero, with a strong breeze.	Ideal for long walks, but remember to take lots of treats and perhaps your water bowl as the puddles and ditches may be frozen over.
3	Heavy rain and thick fog.	Don't worry about the rain (it just runs off fur), but be careful not to lose sight of your housemates who may get lost in the fog. They are likely to be grumpy because they won't want to be walking in the rain.

4	Temperature between 10–15°C with light showers.	Good for playtime with other dogs as both long- and short-haired breeds can enjoy this weather. If you get wet, be sure to wait until you are back in the house before giving yourself a good shake – preferably in the vicinity of one or more of your housemates.
5	Temperature between 15–25°C with occasional cloud.	Care needs to be taken not to overdo your exercising. Stick to shady spots or only leave the house when there is cloud cover. Under no circumstances play with cocker spaniel puppies in this heat: they don't understand the concept of overexercising.
6	Temperature 25–30°C.	Amber warning – long-haired breeds should not venture off a cool flagstone floor. Do not be tempted outside by the promise of treats. Your health is at stake.
7	Temperature 30°C+ with no cloud cover.	Red alert! Consider emigrating – but not to Australia!

If the appropriate number from the scale could be announced with each weather forecast, we puppies would know what it means and could act accordingly. Please give this your serious consideration.

Yours faithfully,

Coco Canine Esquire

PS In order to make sure the correct information gets to all domestic animals, who I'm sure would benefit as much as puppies, perhaps you could consider changing your name to the Pet Office. I'm all for inclusivity (except for cats), so perhaps an overall change of name is going a bit too far; how about a branch for furry friends, far and wide (except cats)? I am a busy puppy, but if you need any advice on setting up the Pet Office, please don't hesitate to get in touch.

Message from Coco to Karen

15th August 2022

Dear Karen,

I begin this letter in a state of despondency. I have just discovered from a streetwise puppy I met while out on a walk today what 'CBA' stands for – and it is no mistake. So not only will I not be receiving an award from the queen, but I am outraged at having such rude, uncouth housemates. I need to remind them that I am a golden retriever and we are *not* a highly strung breed. We are known for being chilled and I feel that I epitomise that characteristic – except, of course, when I'm on the campaign trail, where I am energetic and vocal.

So there is no need to say Coco can't be… no, I refuse to write that word. I am merely conserving my energy for more important things than going for yet another walk.

Actually, I've been giving a certain matter some thought recently. I wonder if, as a leader among my breed, I ought to introduce a motto for other golden retrievers and those who come after us to follow. I have considered several and shortlisted three:

- *Dormiens melius quam exercens* = Sleeping is better than exercising.
- *Ne expendas industria necesse est* = Do not expend energy unnecessarily.
- *Dormiens est ius vitae* = Sleep is the elixir of life.

I like the second one best. It suggests that while we're not short of energy, we use it sparingly and only for the essential things in life, which is a good lesson for puppies everywhere, not just golden retrievers. And especially cocker spaniels! What do you think?

I'm certainly getting my share of fresh sea air. On Saturday, we went to the beach at Gullane and then yesterday we went again to North Berwick. There were lots of dogs in both places and, strangely, they all seemed to be enjoying going into the sea for a swim. I barked at one golden retriever to come out immediately as it was dangerous, but he paid no attention to me.

Karen, I can't understand it. I don't let the water touch my paws, even though my housemates try to entice me in by throwing sticks into the sea – I'm not fooled. There was a sign at the beach saying not to touch dead birds because of avian flu – there may be dead birds floating in the sea. In fact, an article on Poodle said there are thousands of dead gannets in the North Sea and they could touch me without me realising.

Really, I was the only sensible dog on the beach. I just spent most of my time digging holes in the sand and rolling on my back. I finished up looking like a sugary – or, rather, a sandy doughnut. I'm not sure my housemates were very pleased when I left most of the sand in the back of the car.

I'm rather excited by an invitation I've received to spend next weekend in the countryside. It has come from some dear friends whose puppy housemate passed away last year. So it will be my job to provide some canine company and be a constantly cheerful presence, always getting under their feet, inviting them to play when they've got other things they should be getting on with, knocking things off the coffee table with my tail, dribbling water from my bowl all over the floor – generally just being a perfect puppy.

My housemates haven't been invited, just me, which is rather embarrassing, but I suspect they don't make very good house guests. Actually, I'm a touch anxious about it as it is the first time I will have left them on their own overnight and I don't know how they'll manage. If it wasn't for me getting them up and out in the morning, I think they would just stay in bed all day. I'm fully expecting to find them still in their pyjamas when I get home on Sunday.

Lots of love,

Coco x

Message from Coco to Karen

18th August 2022

Dear Karen,

I've had another of those tragic letters (actually, I get quite a few of them), to which I absolutely must reply. The writer sounds positively suicidal, so please could you look over my draft response as quickly as possible to make sure that it is helpful?

Thanks so much,

Coco x

Letter to Coco from Lucky, Received 17th August 2022

Dear Coco,

My name is Lucky and I am a twelve-year old mongrel, so I am very low down in status in the canine community. Perhaps I am being impertinent in even writing to you for advice but I do know that you regard inclusivity as important so I hope that you don't mind.

    I had a very unhappy puppyhood, which is too painful to even think about, but eventually I ended up in a shelter for dogs. And then my wonderful housemates offered me a home when I was two years old. How happy I have been these last ten years. I've enjoyed lots of walks, sausages for my dinner, a comfortable basket, and loads and loads of affection and cuddles. My life has been nothing short of perfect.

    My housemates used to call me Licky Lucky, because I was always giving them kisses, but two weeks ago, it all changed. My housemates came home with a King Charles spaniel puppy called Princess. She is far superior to me – she is pure-bred and registered with The Kennel Club, with a very distinguished lineage. My housemates are constantly cuddling her and playing games with her and she runs around and does daft things to make them laugh.

I feel completely left out. Princess has trashed all my toys and she sometimes sleeps in my basket and eats out of my bowl. My housemates tell me they still love me, but it seems to me that Princess has a special place in their hearts and now that I am old and ugly, they don't want me around anymore. I don't know what to do. I'm so frightened that I am going to be turfed out onto the street and find myself homeless again. On the other hand, maybe I should make it easy for my housemates and just run away.

Your advice would be very welcome, but I will understand if I'm not important enough for you to spend time on. After all, I'm just an old, rather shabby mongrel whose best years are behind her.

Humbly yours,

Lucky

Draft Letter from Coco to Lucky for Karen's Comments

Dear Lucky,

What a wonderful dog you are, providing constant and faithful companionship and affection to your housemates for ten years. They obviously love you dearly, and have done right from the moment they first saw you in the shelter. They have provided you with everything you could possibly ask for and now… they have provided you with a little sister.

Have you thought that perhaps they got the new puppy for you, rather than for themselves? Maybe they feel that you would like to have a friend to keep you company when they are out, another dog to cuddle up with on a winter's evening. Everything in your letter tells me that they still love you and don't want you to be lonely in your old age.

Perhaps they have been a bit thoughtless (I can sympathise, my housemates can be like that, too) in introducing a new puppy so suddenly and spending so much time with her, but puppies need a lot of attention, and gradually, I'm sure Princess will become a regular member of your household and you'll all get on fine together.

But, Lucky, I think there is a deep-rooted problem that has caused this severe bout of anxiety and that is your exceptionally low self-esteem. As you point out in your letter, I am completely committed to inclusivity among dogs, and it is my firm belief that we are all born equal and should be treated with respect and consideration. Just because you are a rescue mongrel does not mean that you are low in status. What it does mean is that you have valuable life experience from which all of us can learn, if you will share it with us.

And that is my advice to you – become a big sister to Princess; adopt the role of mentor and guide. Be gentle but firm when she tries to steal your food, but do welcome her into your basket (if there is room) as she may simply be needing a cuddle. Remember she has just left her mummy and siblings behind and is probably confused by the new routine and surroundings which means she will be very happy to find that she has a new friend who can show her the ropes. It might be a little while before she realises this, but she'll get there eventually.

Chin up, Lucky! Princess and your housemates are fortunate to have a dog of your experience to look up to.

Yours,

Coco

Message from Coco to Karen

25th August 2022

Dear Karen,

Well, I hardly know where to start – there has been so much happening. First of all, I had a great time in the countryside. My hosts couldn't have been kinder. They gave me lots of yummy food and treats and regular tummy tickles. What was even better, when we went out in the car, I got to sit in the back seat with one of them, not in the boot on my own surrounded by wellington boots and shopping bags like I normally do. I felt like a king.

However – as I expected – when I got home, the place was in disarray. My housemates had put away my toys and blankets ('tidying up' they call it) and I had to get them all out again and spread them around to make sure nothing was missing. Luckily for them, everything seems to be there. Still, I'm a bit annoyed with them as it seems they went away for the weekend while I was in the countryside. I overheard them telling friends about their trip to London and how much they had enjoyed it. They went without me! I would have liked to go with them and to visit the House of Commons to lobby for my activist work. So typical of them to go behind my back.

I was no sooner back from the countryside than we were off to visit friends in Dunbar. Now normally, a trip to see friends wouldn't be something I would write to you about, but *these* friends have six cats! Yes, six! And one of them only has three legs.

Well, I was very wary. The cats got hustled out via one door while I entered by another and then we had a contest of who would blink first as we stared at each other through the glass panel separating us. I wasn't going to be intimidated by them so long as there was a door between us, but I certainly wasn't going to confront them in the garden. One or two of them looked rather fierce, and those claws! Lethal. Did you know cats can hide their claws inside their toes, Karen? No, neither did I, until this gathering of felines started flexing theirs in my direction.

When we left the cat house, to my surprise, we didn't go home – I had wondered why my bed and toys were in the car with us. You wouldn't believe it, Karen – we went to stay in a hotel for a couple of nights. I've never been in one before and it was rather posh, but you'll be pleased to hear I behaved impeccably.

The best thing was that at breakfast each morning, the waiter asked what I would like to eat. No prizes for guessing correctly – of course I asked for sausages. And they brought them on a special plate just for me. It was wonderful! I'm presenting my Waggy Tail Award to the hotel as the staff were so thoughtful and made me very happy.

Back to 'auld claes an' porridge' now, but it has been a week full of new experiences.

Lots of love,

Coco x

PS Unbeknown to my housemates, the ride in the back seat of the car while I was in the countryside is in line with my secret plan. You see, I'm starting off (reluctantly) travelling in the boot, then I plan to move up to the back seat. If I behave really well there, I hope to be promoted to the front passenger seat and, before you know it, I'll be in the driver's seat, in control. Nairn, here I come!

Message from Coco to Karen

26th August 2022

Dear Karen,

There's been so much happening, I forgot to thank you for turning round the Lucky draft so quickly. I sent it off straightaway and I've already had a reply from Lucky saying how grateful she is for my advice. She's putting it into practice and the situation has started to improve already.

Anyway, on to other things now. As I informed you well over a month ago, I've given up all hope of becoming a racing driver as I *still* haven't heard back from Andrex. So I've been giving some thought to future career options, of which there are several. You know I value your opinion, so after going through the pros and cons of each, I have jotted down my top ten. See what you think.

1. Guide dog: this is obviously a useful service to people with a sensory disability and one to which golden retrievers are particularly well suited due to our calm, serene and caring nature. It has the advantage

of providing constant companionship, which is very attractive. However, it has two big minuses:
- guide dogs are volunteers; they only get bed and board, but no salary. I think I need a job that will provide an income, so I can afford to travel to Nairn regularly as well as fund my lobbying activities;
- the training period is long and it's residential. I rather enjoy living where I do and I'm not sure that I want to move away. My housemates would get lonely and might even get another puppy to replace me. I wouldn't like that.

2. Police dog: again, a worthwhile job and one that would require a high level of commitment. However, I think this might be one of those reserved occupations – when you see police dogs, they're invariably German shepherds who are a lot fiercer and meaner than me. I'm not sure criminals would find me very frightening. I haven't even learned to growl properly yet.

    Also, the work might sometimes require me to put my life on the line and that's rather a scary thought. But I would get a uniform, which is a big plus – I'm told by the streetwise dogs in Edinburgh that lady pups go weak at the knees when they see a guy in uniform. It might also mean, if I'm successful, that I could qualify for a bravery award. Mmm, I'll have to think about that one.

3. The armed forces: while we're on the subject of uniforms, what about if I joined the army? That could be very exciting. Soldiers recruit dogs for all sorts of

jobs, like patrolling, tracking and guarding. I've even heard of dogs being trained to parachute and abseil and carry messages behind enemy lines.

Oh, it would definitely be an adventurous life, but I would have to leave home and probably live in barracks with lots of other dogs. I wonder if I'd be allowed to take my toys with me – probably not. Not even the squeaky bear I like so much.

I don't know if I would be very good on the parade ground either. I get distracted easily and could get into dreadful trouble with the sergeant major and be made to do a hundred press-ups as punishment. No, I'll have to rule out that one.

4. Search and rescue dog: since there are so many hills where I live and I would prefer to work from home, I could explore this idea. At least in Scotland, this is not a profession reserved for St. Bernards. It would mean being out in all weathers, which I don't mind too much, although climbing hills looking for lost people could be quite exhausting. I'd be good at digging them out of the snow, though, and I could carry a flask of brandy round my neck (perhaps it's whisky in Scotland). That's a possibility.

5. Airport sniffer dog: I do have a very sensitive nose – I can smell sausages from a hundred metres – so perhaps this would be a good choice. I am sure I would get training to detect drugs and explosives, but I could add to my CV that I can sniff out illicit foodstuffs as well. I wonder if I'd get to eat any of the food I find.

6. Farm dog: I'm not sure why I'm putting this one down because, to be honest, it's a bit energetic for me and probably reserved for Border collies anyway. Sheep are pretty stupid animals and running around after them all day would be tiresome. All the farm dogs I've met have to sleep in kennels outside and they don't have a lovely cosy basket like I do. On the plus side, I would get to travel by tractor and Land Rover and I'd enjoy that. I might even get a shot on a quad bike. That would be fun.

7. Human walker: these dogs provide a service to humans who are on their own all day, staying at home and not taking enough exercise. I should give serious thought to this option as according to a Poodle search, exercise is an invaluable tool in the fight against obesity and diabetes. No, Karen, I don't think they are antisocial neighbours; I know they are nasty conditions that afflict humans. And yes, I do now know that Covid is a virus. I don't appreciate you not bothering to put me right on that little faux pas.

    Of course, I would have to be selective about which humans I walked. I'd only take those who could be trusted to walk off the lead without running away and would come to me when I bark at them. I wouldn't want any naughty people.

8. Therapy pet: one of my housemates suggested this, because I'm so cuddly and friendly. I would visit people in care homes or children who are poorly in hospital. I like being fussed over and having my tummy tickled, so I definitely have the right temperament, and there would be a high level of job satisfaction.

Unfortunately, like guide dogs, I think it's probably a voluntary position and I really need the money. Also, I would need to declare my flatulence attack in the old people's home, as I'm sure there are stringent checks done on therapy dogs. It's probably a non-starter, but worthy of consideration.

9. Film star: please don't laugh, Karen. I'm serious. Other dogs, like Lassie and Marley, have made it onto the big screen, so why shouldn't I? I'd need to take a screen test, of course, and be able to take instruction from the director, but I see no reason why I couldn't become a Hollywood icon. Don't you think it's time that a golden retriever was awarded a Golden Globe, when it is so obviously named after us?

10. Stud: this is a freelance occupation, but with my looks, I wouldn't have any difficulty in getting work. I'd have to check first with Milly to make sure that she doesn't mind. Just one minor obstacle – my testicles still haven't dropped.

So, there we are. It's such a varied list with different working conditions and skills required. Which do you think I would be best suited to? My housemates say there is no rush for me to find work and they are happy to provide for my needs, but I think I should be looking ahead and making plans.

Lots of love,

Coco x

Message from Coco to Karen

30th August 2022

Dear Karen,

I am outraged – spitting tacks, I'm so angry. Out of the goodness of my heart, I agreed to participate in a survey of puppies who had been placed in their home in the last three months. I filled in the questionnaire truthfully with the best of intentions.

Unknown to me, my housemates (who, tellingly, opted to remain anonymous) were also asked to fill it in. They thought I wouldn't see it, but I have and I'm sending you a copy with this letter. Some of the things they refer to, like needing to go out at 5am, are from when I was younger. Now, I sleep right through to 7am.

The hypocrisy! They can't tell me to my face that I am a wonderful dog and then, behind my back, say things about me that are not even true. What do you think I should do? Should I confront them and tell them that I know about their disloyalty and duplicity?

In a rage.

Love,

Coco x

Coco's Three-Month Probation Period Assessment

	Characteristics of a Perfect Puppy	Coco's Assessment		Housemates' Assessment	
		Score out of 10	Comments	Score out of 10	Comments
1	Confident	5	I'm really quite a shy puppy, especially around girls. It's just that I act macho.	12	Coco is inclined to be overconfident and tackles things he is not yet ready for – e.g. going upstairs, when he is not able to get down again. Then, he gets stuck and goes nuts.
2	Friendly	10	I'm super-friendly with everyone.	8	Coco is very friendly, but is not always able to assess whether others want to be friends with him. Examples include older, grumpy dogs and those strange people who are not dog-lovers.

3	Tidy	10	My bed and garden are a delight, full of carefully selected and gently nurtured items. Anything unwanted is buried or chewed apart.	3	Coco is lucky to score three for this category. His bed and garden would be a disaster area if we didn't constantly tidy up after him.
4	A pleasure to live with	10	I really can't think of a better house companion. I bring constant delight to everyone around me.	9	Ninety per cent of the time Coco is a wonderful companion – we would prefer not to comment on the other ten per cent for fear of litigation.
5	Obedient	N/a	I don't recognise this as a necessary characteristic.	7	Coco generally goes along with what we want to do. However, he has been known to refuse to go on walks or get in and out of the car. Occasionally, he doesn't come when he is called, especially if he has found something particularly rotten to chew on or is enjoying playing with other dogs.

6	Always toilets in the correct place	10	Wherever I choose to toilet is the correct place to toilet.	8	Coco has always toileted outside, but not always in the designated area. He now considers the flower bed immediately beside the front door his en-suite toilet, which it definitely is not.
7	Never an embarrassment	10	I can't think of a single instance when I might have been an embarrassment.	4	Note his gaseous attack in the old people's home, which he has forbidden us to mention (please don't let him know that we referred to it or he'll be furious with us and make our lives miserable for days).
8	Never 'borrows' housemates' belongings	10	I like to adopt the attitude 'What's mine is theirs and what's theirs is mine'. We share everything harmoniously. If my housemates want to play with my toys, eat out of my bowls or sleep in my bed, that's fine by me.	2	Coco seems to think that all of the shoes and slippers in the house belong to him and we are constantly having to retrieve our belongings from the garden. These include a spectacle case with spectacles in it, doorstops, drink mats and baseball caps.

9	Sleeps soundly	10	I sleep the sleep of the just.	9	Coco sleeps well – it's just a pity he likes to have an enormous drink of water immediately before he settles down at night and then needs to be let out at 5am.
10	Cuddly	10	Cuddling is a very important part of my day and I'm rather good at it.	9	Coco's cuddles would be better if he stopped trying to surreptitiously eat our sleeves while he's doing it.
	TOTAL	85		71	

Coco added two extra lines:

11	Good-looking	10+	This is a very important attribute as people stop to admire me and thus I expand my housemates' circle of friends and acquaintances in the local area.
12	Modest	10	I don't like to brag about my many attributes, but they are plain for all to see.

Revised total: 105+

Signed: **Coco**
Signed: Anonymous

Message from Coco to Karen

2nd September 2022

Dear Karen,

You are always so understanding and give such good advice. I wish my housemates were more like you.

Of course you are right; maybe there have been times when my behaviour hasn't been absolutely perfect, but I do always try to please. In future, I'll get permission from my housemates before I take their stuff and I'll co-operate with them on getting in and out of the car – I am perfectly able to go up and down the steps, I just find it amusing when they have to lift up my bottom to get me in. They make such a fuss about it.

Now to a different topic you'll be pleased to hear that I have bought a present for one of my housemates, who will have her birthday on Saturday. I put a lot of thought into what to get her because I want her to know that I love her, even though she's not always perfect either.

So, I've got her a small selection of things. First of all, a packet of chicken-flavoured treats. I know she's vegetarian, but she'll love them all the same. Actually, I had to buy two packets as I ate the first one. In fact, I've eaten most of the second one as well. I can't afford to buy a third packet as I've spent all my money now, so I've taped across the top where I tore it open and it looks as though it's untouched. It's just a pity that there are only five treats left in the bottom of the packet, when it says 'Pack of 25' on the front. Hopefully she won't notice as I've tried to score out the '2'. I just couldn't resist.

Do you think she'll share the remaining treats with me?

Secondly, I've bought her a shiny, bouncy blue ball. She will so enjoy playing with it and maybe I can play with her. I thought I should test out its bounciness before I wrapped it up and it really is lovely and squidgy. Unfortunately, after I'd played with it a bit, I noticed that I had inadvertently left some teeth marks on it. I don't think she'll mind; I can just say that it happened while I was wrapping it.

And my third present is the best of all – three tickets for the Paws at the Palace event at Scone Palace on Sunday, the day after her birthday. The advertisement says there will be lots of doggy fun and games, parades of different breeds, agility classes and demonstrations. Also, there will be stalls selling treats and gifts for puppies. I can't wait!

Oh, I've just thought – she will use one of the tickets for me, won't she?

On tenterhooks!

Lots of love,

Coco x

Message from Coco to Karen

5th September 2022

Dear Karen,

Whew! I got one of the tickets; what a relief.

It was great fun. There were so many dogs there and I think I introduced myself to most of them. We went round all the stalls and my housemates treated me to a pup cake. Oh, it was so delicious and had bacon on the top for decoration. I'll drop some hints and see if we can make them at home. Perhaps I should write to the Earl of Mansfield, who lives at Scone Palace, and see if he will send me the recipe.

Disappointingly, we didn't take home any rosettes. We had thought we might enter the puppy and housemate lookalike competition, but we realised when we saw some of the other entrants that we wouldn't stand a chance: an Old English sheepdog with her hair done up in a topknot just like her housemate and a bulldog accompanied by a bald bodybuilder. They were like two peas in a pod.

I'm still giving a great deal of thought to my future career and I have to admit that I agree with you – none of the ones

I've considered so far is quite right for me. So I've taken your advice and tried to be more analytic – looking at my strengths and my requirements for job satisfaction. Here's my list:

Strengths:
Caring, thoughtful, considerate, articulate, handsome, glass half-full and sometimes positively brimming over.

Requirements:
Living wage+, work from home, high level of job satisfaction, time to continue as an activist, regular meal breaks and frequent sleep breaks.

What do you think? Does anything spring to mind?

My housemates and I have begun watching *Dogs Behaving Badly* on Channel Five. It's supposed to be a programme about dysfunctional households where the dog and the housemates have behavioural problems. A very understanding TV presenter then goes to their home to try to resolve them. Although it's quite interesting, I feel rather aggrieved by the title – it is totally mis-named. It's plain to see that it should be called *Housemates Behaving Badly*. All the advice is about changing the behaviour of the housemates and then everything improves. The dogs are all entirely blameless.

Fortunately, we don't have any behavioural problems here in our house.

Lots of love,

Coco x

Letter from Coco to Scone Palace, Perthshire

6th September 2022

Dear Lord Mansfield,

May I say how much I enjoyed the canine event at Scone Palace last weekend. I brought my two housemates with me and they had a lovely time – there were plenty of things for them to do and other humans with whom they could mingle.

One of the highlights of the day for me, personally, was the rather delicious pup cake that I bought from your cafeteria. Would you be so kind as to share the recipe with me? My housemates have agreed to help me bake some if we can get a list of ingredients and the instructions. I hope the recipe is not patented, but if it is, please consider making an exception for me as I get very few treats and this is a rare opportunity.

Yours humbly,

Coco Canine Esquire

Message from Coco to Karen

7th September 2022

Dear Karen,

I spoke too soon about behavioural problems, or lack thereof. I've felt for some time that trouble was brewing and, sure enough, I have a problem with my housemates.

You see, they have always been very clingy, wanting to be with me all the time and feeling unhappy if I'm not within sight. But now it appears to have developed into full-blown separation anxiety. Every time I leave them for even a little while to pursue one of my own special interests, such as the hole I'm digging in the back garden that they haven't discovered yet, I can hear them calling to me in such plaintive tones – "Coco, Coco, where are you?" – that I immediately have to drop everything and rush back to the house to reassure them that I haven't abandoned them.

Take yesterday, for example: I had just gone next door to spend some time with our equine neighbours, Mick and Coco, and I'd only been there a few minutes when I heard my housemates calling to me in the distance with a rising note of panic in their voices. I was reluctant to go home, so I lingered for a bit longer with the ponies, but then the housemates came rushing round the corner. They let out big sighs of relief when they realised I had been there all the time.

This sort of behaviour was all right when I was still a small puppy and not venturing far, but it's unacceptable now that I'm six months old and needing to get out and about more. I really can't have my life constrained in this way, so I'm exploring therapy for them – it's the only answer. In fact, I have resolved to write to Channel Five and ask if *Dogs (Housemates) Behaving Badly* will send the relationship expert to sort them out. In the meantime, if you hear of anyone who might be able to help, then please let me know.

On a much happier note, I've just received the most wonderful present from Milly – a photograph of herself, curled up asleep. She looks positively adorable and I'm going to attach it to the side of my bed so that she is the last thing I see before I go to sleep at night and the first thing I see when I wake up in the morning. She is my pin-up!

Only two days now before I see her in the flesh and no Covid to upset our plans this time, I hope. I've bought a present to take to her – some special treats containing camomile, which is supposed to have a calming effect. I'm hoping that, along with my own bodybuilding exercises, the energy drinks and the double espressos, it will mean I might just make it through the weekend without collapsing from exhaustion.

I'll let you know. Wish me luck.

Lots of love,

Coco x

Letter from Coco to Channel Five

8th September 2022

Dear Chief Executive,

May I start by saying how much I enjoy your programme *Dogs Behaving Badly*. It is so accurate in highlighting the bad habits of human housemates and getting puppy/human relations back on track. The dogs you work with must be extremely grateful.

As I watch it regularly, it crossed my mind that my housemates and I could perhaps participate in one of your episodes as we have a particular problem that your expert mediator may be able to resolve. You see, I'm an adventurous sort of dog and my housemates are rather timid, stay-at-home types. When I am running after deer in the woods or chasing squirrels, it sends them into paroxysms of anxiety in case they lose sight of me. They have become very emotionally dependent and find it difficult to function without my constant presence, to the extent that I really don't know how they managed before I came to live here. As I'm sure you can imagine, I find this quite burdensome and I am seeking therapy for them to bolster their confidence so that I may enjoy a greater degree of freedom.

If you think we would make a good case study, then please get in touch. I should add that while I am extremely photogenic, my housemates are less so. However, nothing so bad that an intensive session with your make-up and wardrobe departments couldn't put right.

I look forward to hearing from you,

Coco Canine Esquire

PS In case you are considering using a canine adviser to work on the programme to make it more dog-friendly (e.g. changing the title to reflect its objectives more accurately), then please bear in mind that I am available, for a modest fee, to help out.

Message from Coco to Karen

12th September 2022

Dear Karen,

Oh, it was wonderful. Two whole days with Milly. I can't begin to tell you how much fun we had together. We played in the garden, we played on the beach, we played in the house – it was non-stop enjoyment. We even shared our dinner from the same bowl. So romantic, don't you agree?

You'll be pleased to hear that I was very gallant and allowed Milly to have first dibs at the food, then I joined her after a few minutes. I couldn't help noticing, however, that she took all of the tasty bits for herself, so there was no chicken or tuna by the time I got my turn, just biscuity stuff. I was a bit disappointed because I was rather hungry after all that exercise, but naturally I forgave her. After all, she needs to eat more so that she can grow – she's still just a wee scrap of a thing, even if she is extraordinarily energetic. Perhaps if she didn't run around so much, more of the calories could go into growth. I think that's why I've got so big – I make sure not to overdo it.

I was a bit alarmed on Saturday morning, I can tell you. It appears that Milly has a couple of friends – the 'Boys Next Door', she calls them. They are two enormous Gordon Setters called Frank and Hugo. At first, I was concerned that they might have designs on my Milly, but it seems not; the friendships are purely platonic. In fact, given the interest that one of the Setters showed in me, I rather think he may be a Gay Gordon.

So I'm a bit sad today that Milly and I are once again apart, but I'm taking the opportunity to regain my strength and get to the shops to restock on energy drinks. I'm not sure when we'll see each other again, but I've promised to write and I hope that way she won't forget about me. She has quite a few doggy friends in Nairn, so I mustn't flag in pressing my suit.

Off for a snooze now to allow my tired muscles to recover.

Lots of love,

Coco x

Letter from Coco to Milly, Nairn

13th September 2022

Dearest, darling Milly,

Thank you so much for a wonderful weekend, I enjoyed every minute of it. I hope it won't be long before we can get together again. You'll be pleased to hear that the wound on my ear, where you nipped it, is healing nicely and I don't think there will be a scar on my nose where you scratched me with your claw.

I hope your puppy training classes are going well and will help you to be less frantic. While it's not a condition that I suffer from personally, I do find that having my housemates give me a facial or a back rub is wonderfully soothing and relaxing. Perhaps you could ask your housemates to do the same, but you would have to sit still while they did it, so that would be tricky.

Back here in Perthshire I'm rather lonely now – just me and my housemates. There is talk of us getting together at Christmas – I poodled Christmas and it's three months away. That's ages!

Apparently, the night before Christmas, some fat chap with a white beard comes down the chimney. Hah! I'd like to see him try. There's also usually a lot of meat on offer – turkey, goose, ham, and sausages wrapped in bacon (heavenly) – which sounds much more my kind of thing. My tummy is rumbling in anticipation – of seeing you and sharing the meat, of course, but three months seems a very long time to wait, so I'm working on my housemates to fix up a playdate before then and to get in some sausages to tide me over. If they'll wrap them in bacon, even better.

Meanwhile, please find enclosed a recipe for pup cakes that I think you will rather enjoy. I've made them myself, so can heartily recommend them. It's an old family recipe from one of the landed gentry, whose name I can't divulge. Let me know how you get on baking them.

Please don't forget about me because you don't see me regularly. I remain your most loyal friend and suitor.

Lots of love,

Coco x

PS I have sent my condolences to the royal corgis. They must be so sad at the passing of their majestic housemate.

Recipe for Pup Cakes

Ingredients:
- 165g self-raising flour
- 165g finely grated carrot
- 1 medium banana, mashed
- 2 eggs
- 60ml honey

To decorate:
- 280g cream cheese
- 12 strips of streaky bacon

Method:
- Preheat your oven to 170°C (325°F/gas mark 3) and grease a mini muffin tray.
- Beat together all ingredients until well mixed (Milly, at this stage, it is very helpful to taste the mixture a few times just in case it needs a bit of adjusting e.g. not sweet enough, in which case add another dollop of honey).
- Place a teaspoon of mixture into each muffin cup (Milly, I suggest not being too thorough in scraping the mixture out of the bowl or off the spoon, as you

may want to lick both items once the cakes are in the oven).
- Bake for twenty-five mins and then leave to cool completely before removing from the tin (Milly, this bit is nonsense, really. I find that it is necessary to taste at least one of them as soon as they are out of the oven, just to make sure that they have cooked enough).
- Fry the strips of bacon (I suggest increasing the amount from twelve to fifteen to allow for a bit of 'evaporation', if you know what I mean).
- Whip the cream cheese until smooth and then spread onto the pup cakes.
- Decorate each one with a bacon strip (Milly, it says that this will make twelve mini pup cakes, but, personally, I find that I rarely end up with more than eight).

Message from Coco to Karen

19th September 2022

Dear Karen,

Well, I suppose it's the time of year, but I am overwhelmed by a positive deluge of letters from unhappy dogs asking me for advice. What's the problem? I needed to poodle it, so you may ask. Yes, it's the start of the academic year.

Why should that be causing problems in the canine community (apart from the fact that its members are unfairly barred from enrolling at university)? Here is a typical letter that explains all. I've drafted my response, so please let me know what you think – two heads are always better than one.

Dear Coco,

I am in a state of profound shock. Just composing this letter is plunging me back into the depths of despair, but I must share my feelings with someone who can understand them.

You see, I came to live here with my housemates when I was just an eight-week old Beagle puppy. In fact, I arrived in my home on the thirteenth birthday of the youngest boy of the household. He and I have been best friends ever since and we have done everything together. We have played all sorts of games, gone swimming in the river, made sandcastles at the beach (I dug the moat while he and his little sister made the turrets) and shared a bed.

He always smuggled some tasty titbits from the kitchen table for me and brushed my coat if it got muddy. When I had to go to the vet, which I don't enjoy, he would come with me and comfort me. If he got into trouble, I was always there for him. We were inseparable. While he was at school, I would just have a sleep and a mooch round the garden and then the fun would start as soon as he came home again. It's been this way for six years and I couldn't have been happier.

But now… well, now he has gone off to university in a town a hundred miles away and he will stay there and not come home each day to be with me. It will be weeks and weeks before I see him again. I feel bereaved and I can't understand why he has done this. There is a university in our town, but he has chosen not to go to it because it doesn't offer veterinary medicine. Surely if he loved me as much as I love him, he would have found a course there.

My other housemates can see that I am very unhappy and are trying to comfort me, especially his little sister, but it's not the same as having my best friend here with me. I sleep on our bed each night and wake up alone in the morning in a state of total despondency. What am I to do?

Please advise as soon as possible.

Buddy

Draft Letter from Coco to Buddy

Dear Buddy,

Thank you so much for writing to me and expressing the inconsolable grief that you and other dogs are experiencing at the start of the academic year. I can understand the wrench you must feel at being parted from your best friend, but, I wonder, might it be because of you that he has gone away to study veterinary medicine?

You see, being with you all the time must have made him realise how special dogs are and now he would like to devote his life to making sure that they are healthy and well cared for. He may also be thinking that, in future years, you may need to make use of his expertise in canine medicine. He will be there to help you if you fall ill or suffer from the ailments of old age, rather than you having to go to the vet you mention, visits to whom you yourself say you dislike.

In other words – you are his inspiration. Helping him to find his path in life and then supporting him along that path is one of the very best things you could do for your friend.

Of course, while I realise that this may bring a warm glow and a sense of pride to your heart, it is unlikely to diminish the abandonment you currently feel. You mention that his little sister is concerned about you and is doing her best to help you through it. My guess is that she is also missing your friend because he sounds like he is a wonderful big brother to her. How about if you focus more attention on her and give her some comfort in return, in case she too is feeling lonely? I realise she can't replace your friend, but she may be able to offer some of the companionship you are missing.

And remember, the university holidays are long. A Poodle search will tell you all you need to know. Before you can blink, he will be back home to have fun with you again. Because – of this I am sure – he will be missing you just as much as you are missing him. Take heart, Buddy, there are still plenty of fun times ahead. You just have to be a little bit patient.

Your brother,

Coco

Message from Coco to Karen

24th September 2022

Dear Karen,

Please could you prepare a bed for me back at the farm? I fear I may have to return. I'm in dreadful trouble with my housemates – through no fault of my own, I should add.

You see, they decided we should take up foraging, so that we can live off the land around us and become more self-sufficient. Well, I thought it was a daft idea, but decided to go along with it – just to humour them.

This morning, one of my housemates and I were out with our basket collecting mushrooms, brambles, herbs and so forth. It was no fun at all; I don't even like mushrooms – horrible, slimy, slippery things. I was about to go home and leave him to it when we turned a corner of the lane and… bonanza! At last, something worth collecting – a real, live chicken.

Of course, it ran for its life, clucking and shrieking, when it saw me, but I set off in pursuit. I could see or hear nothing else and in my mind were images of chicken hotpot, chicken and bacon pie, roast chicken with all the trimmings and maybe even a Saturday night chicken vindaloo.

At last, I cornered it between a shed and a wall, grabbed it and took it triumphantly back to my housemate. It was only then that I realised he was screaming blue murder at me and threatening me with all sorts of dire consequences if I didn't release the chicken. Of course, I wasn't to be fooled. He just wanted to deprive me of the kudos of having caught it and take all the glory for himself. It would be, by far, the best thing in the basket. So, I pranced around, showing it off, just out of arm's reach.

Eventually, I realised that he really was very angry with me, so I dropped the chicken, which ran away back to its coop. *There goes my chicken dinner*, I thought. We were a very sober pair returning home joined together by the lead.

When we got back, he recounted the story to my other housemate and she looked very disappointed in me. I took myself off to a corner of the sitting room and kept a low profile for ten minutes or so, until it had all blown over. I think we're OK again now, but keep that bed handy just in case I have to return.

Boring old biscuity stuff for dinner tonight, I suppose. Shame, a tasty chicken thigh would have gone down a treat.

Love,

Coco x

Postcard from Coco to Karen

28th September 2022

Dear Karen,

Greetings from the beautiful island of Colonsay. I have come here on holiday with my housemates. The weather is glorious and I am in and out of the sea all day long. This is the life!

Wish you were here,

Coco x

Message from Coco to Karen

1st October 2022

Dear Karen,

Home again. Sand everywhere – in my coat, in the car, in my water bowl. But oh, it was worth it.

You know, this holiday was the first time I had been on the high seas and you would have been so proud of me – I wasn't even the tiniest bit seasick on the ferry and I was prepared, at a moment's notice, to take over from the captain if he felt queasy. I might have had a bit of trouble with doing the announcements in Gaelic, but I'm sure I could have got one of the crew to help me out.

My housemates and I had watched *Titanic* on the television a few days before leaving, so I knew what to do in the event of hitting an iceberg – I don't think you get many of those off the west coast of Scotland, but you never can tell, what with global warming and everything. Unfortunately, there wasn't the opportunity to practise putting on a life jacket or jumping into one of the lifeboats, but I'm sure I could have done it, no bother.

Anyway, I'm becoming increasingly well-travelled. Now I've been to two islands, because while we were on Colonsay, we walked over the Strand to Oronsay. I got very wet on the crossing, but I don't mind that now; I've become a bit of an old sea dog. My Edinburgh friends wouldn't have recognised me.

Off to the vet on Monday, so I'm looking forward to seeing Jan and getting a few more cuddles and treats.

Love,

Coco x

Message from Coco to Karen

8th October 2022

Dear Karen,

I'm sorry it's been a while since I last wrote – you see, I've been under the surgeon's knife. What a shock!

In my last letter I mentioned that I was off to see the vet. Well, my housemates left me with Jan and she took me to some kennels, which was fine as there were some other dogs to play with. Then, I felt a bit sleepy, so I lay down and closed my eyes.

The next thing I knew I was waking up and everything was a bit fuzzy. I felt so disorientated and a bit sore between my back legs. My housemates came to collect me and take me home, which I was very pleased about as I don't think I could have got there on my own. That's when they broke the news to me that I will never be a daddy because I can't sire pups. To be honest, I felt so horrible and woozy that I didn't care; I just wanted to sleep on my own blankets and wait for the soreness to go away.

My housemates didn't tell me beforehand because they

didn't want me to worry, but if I hadn't had the operation I might have become very ill, so I'm glad it's all over and done with. I've had a horrible time and today is really the first day I've felt well enough to write to you. To add insult to injury, I have to wear a collar that looks like a lampshade round my head. Now that I'm feeling better and ready to have fun again, this is a real nuisance. Jan says it may be several more days before I can take it off.

You know what a sociable puppy I am. Well, I'm not going to go anywhere in public wearing this ridiculous lampshade – it's all too embarrassing. I'll just play in the garden instead and avoid company.

Actually, I don't mind never being a daddy. Raising pups must be terribly time-consuming and I've got so much going on. I would rather be an uncle to many than father to a few. However, I will have to break the news to Milly, but maybe not until she's a bit older.

I have to admit that there have been one or two good things happening as a result of the operation. First of all, my housemates are giving me the best meals you can think of – all my favourites: sausages, ham and chicken. I was a bit off my food immediately after the operation, but now my appetite has come roaring back and I'm loving my meals.

Secondly, one of my housemates is sleeping downstairs with me in the sitting room. We call it 'the boys' dorm' and we do enjoy ourselves. One evening, after lying in bed watching *Marley* (again) on the television, we were both feeling a bit peckish. So, we had a midnight feast. Scrummy.

He says we can only do this while I'm convalescing – that means recovering, I had to look it up in the dogtionary

– after which he'll move back upstairs again to sleep. So I'm going to have to keep my hangdog expression for as long as possible. It's a bit difficult when I'm having fun playing with my toys.

Love,

Coco x

PS Karen, did you know that the expression 'good as gold' is actually short for 'good as a golden retriever'? I didn't realise it either, but it's entirely logical.

Message from Coco to Karen

11th October 2022

Dear Karen,

You are a genius. You really are. Why did I not see it myself?

Of course, my ideal career is agony uncle. It's so obvious and meets all my criteria. In fact, my career has pretty much begun already as I'm still getting letters from puppies in distress. I attach the latest one and my draft response. See what you think.

Now that I've settled on a career path (so, so, so excited), I'll start to put together a portfolio of my work to show to doggie magazines to see if they might be interested in taking me on. Of course, I'll need to compose a very carefully worded covering letter. I'll send you a draft of that too once I've written it.

Bear in mind that I don't want to get typecast solely as an agony uncle, but I do feel that if I could get a paw in the door, other opportunities in the media might open up. For example, perhaps it could lead to becoming an investigative journalist – going undercover to expose criminal gangs or political shenanigans. I've already made a start on the latter too – as Dilyn found to his cost. Or I could double up as a restaurant critic – sharing all my experiences of dining in the finest establishments and receiving five-star treatment. Being so photogenic, I expect I'll receive requests to contribute to the beauty and well-being pages, and there's always the role of features editor if there are stories to be told about famous puppies (apart from me) and their adventurous lives.

Oh, the opportunities are endless. I can't wait to get started.

Wish me luck.

Love,

Coco x

PS Karen, please could you help me with something? You see, I love running into Loch Tay to fetch sticks and things – we go there a lot. My housemates try to encourage me to swim, but I don't do it because I'm not really sure how it works. Do I just take my paws off the bottom and float? How exactly does one doggy paddle? What will happen if a big wave comes? Will I get washed away? Please advise asap.

Letter to Coco (as Agony Uncle)

9th October 2022

Dear Coco,

My name is Butter (short for Butterfly) and I am a three-year-old papillon. I live in a lovely flat with my housemate, Sophie. When I came to live here, Sophie was single and carefree and took me everywhere with her. We were never apart, not for an instant.

Sad to say, this golden period appears to have come to an end. In the summer, she met a man (not good enough for her, in my opinion) and now he is often hanging around the flat, getting in the way. Although he pretends to like me I know he doesn't, as he often growls at me when he thinks Sophie can't hear.

When he's not hanging around and getting under my paws, he likes her to go with him to the cinema or to a football match and I get left behind on my own. Worst of all, he says that I shouldn't be allowed to share a bed with her and should be made to sleep in the sitting room. I mean, whose house does he think this is? His? He doesn't seem to like me sitting at the end of the bed watching them intently when they are – you know – getting a bit intimate.

I have to find a way of getting rid of this fellow. What would you suggest? So long as it's (more or less) legal and not too much blood (his) is spilt, I'm prepared to consider anything.

Eagerly awaiting your reply,

Butter (wouldn't melt in my mouth)

Draft Reply from Coco to Butter

10th October 2022

Dear Butter,

I do hope we can resolve your situation without resorting to violence, but I can see that you are up for it if necessary. As a peace-loving creature myself, I would prefer to look at a couple of options that don't involve bloodshed.

First of all, as you have enjoyed the longer relationship with Sophie, I can't help thinking that you are in the stronger position. If you agree with that, then we can take advantage of it. Would you agree that Sophie would be appalled if she thought that her boyfriend had been cruel to you on the sly? And would she be bound to take your side? If so, I suggest you practise 'quaking'.

Allow me to elaborate. As soon as he arrives at the flat, start quivering and shaking, and run to hide behind a piece of furniture. Stay there until he has gone and do not, under any circumstances, be tempted out by treats or endearments. Be strong, Butter! Once he has left, rush to Sophie and snuggle up to her as though you are seeking comfort. You have to do this as often as it takes to get Sophie to believe that you are terrified of the boyfriend, thereby sowing the seed of suspicion that he may have behaved badly towards you and that you can't co-exist.

If you behave in this way and Sophie stops dating him, it may, of course, make her rather sad because she probably enjoys having a boyfriend, although it's obviously not as rewarding as having a loyal, loving dog. So, the next stage in the plan is for you to help Sophie find a new boyfriend; one who likes dogs a lot and will be thrilled to have you as a new friend, too.

The best way to do this is to focus on the dog-owning community. Get Sophie to take you for walks at your local park and when you see a man with a nice dog who looks like he would be just right for Sophie, run up to him and play with the dog. Dance around at his feet looking as cute as possible and do not go back to Sophie when she calls. This will mean that she has to come over to get you and will inevitably engage in conversation with the man. Romance may blossom.

Now, Butter, this may take several attempts as some men are already in a long-term relationship, some are gay and some are happy being single. You will just have to persevere and be as discerning as possible. But if our plan succeeds, then you may be able to open up a new chapter in Sophie's life and make a couple of new friends yourself. Personally, I would suggest that any men walking with a golden retriever would be a good bet – target them.

Butter, I hope you find my advice helpful. Please, under no circumstances, do not attack Sophie's boyfriend, even though, with your spirit and determination, I can't help feeling that he would come off worse.

Best wishes,

Coco

Message from Coco to Karen

24th October 2022

Dear Karen,

Good news! I've got the all-clear. Jan the vet has given me a clean bill of health and I'm back on top form. However, I don't want any more brushes with the surgeon's scalpel, thank you. One was enough.

This means I have been able to stop wearing the lampshade collar, which is just as well as I've trashed two of them already, what with running around in the undergrowth, rolling in the grass cuttings and playing with my toys. This is a bit unfortunate as they cost money, but my housemates are so pleased to see me happy again that they say they don't mind. They patched the collars together with parcel tape and made rather a poor job of it, I have to say. Still, it was good of them to try. However, I couldn't possibly have gone out in public looking like a tramp with sticking plaster round my neck.

That's the good news. The bad news is that when Jan weighed me, she said I had put on two kilos during my three-week convalescence and that I needed to shed some of it. It's true – I have been eating like a king and, of course, I wasn't getting so much exercise immediately after my op. I had to build up my strength. My housemates have put me on a diet, which is one thing, but I wish they would stop calling me Porky. Body shaming is so unkind. They rather fancy themselves as being woke, but it doesn't seem that way to me.

Thank you for the advice about how to swim. Now that I'm fighting fit again, I'll be able to put it into practice. I might borrow my housemate's goggles – I don't like to get splashes of water in my eyes.

Some much-needed good political news this week, and a huge relief for me: Dilyn is definitely not getting back into Number 10 and, with any luck, he will not be getting a knighthood or peerage either. I couldn't stop worrying that he would wriggle his way into the House of Lords, and sabotage the Votes for Puppies campaign. Instead, the political wilderness beckons him.

Life is good!

Love,

Coco x

Message from Coco to Karen

27th October 2022

Dear Karen,

Just back from a short trip to Banchory, where we stayed in a lovely hotel that had sausages on the breakfast menu. They were so delicious I wolfed them down before my housemates could bring up the subject of my diet. Blow that! A lot of burping ensued, but I didn't care.

We went for walks along the River Dee and I tried to follow your advice about doggy-paddling, but I couldn't quite get the hang of it. I'll keep practising though, as you suggested, and I'm sure it'll come to me eventually.

Meanwhile, I wonder if you could settle a dispute between me and my housemates. It's about how to interpret what they say to me. For example, when they call, "Come!" I take it to mean, "Coco, if it's OK with you, and in your own time, no rush, please think about coming to join us." However, they say it is a command and I must come immediately and not dilly-dally.

Similarly, when they say "Stay", I interpret that as

meaning, "Coco, you're not obliged to sit down where you are, so do feel free to wander about in the vicinity and explore any interesting smells." But they tell me I must stay rooted to the spot when I hear them say that. What the housemates say to me is surely meant merely as suggestions for me to consider and I should give them a great deal of thought before acting on them. After all, I don't want to rush into anything I'm not sure of, do I? A critical factor is, of course, the quality of the treats on offer if I do as they say.

Well, I've always been a bit of a sceptic when it comes to astrology, but I'm going to have to rethink that position. You see, having been born on the 6th of March, I'm a Piscean. Yesterday, I thought I would look on Poodle to see what the characteristics of a person born under the sign of Pisces are and – holy moly! They described me to a T. I was completely taken aback.

The website said that a Piscean born on the 6th of March is a free spirit who refuses to conform (as I've said before, I do like to follow my muse). It also said that I am inspirational and might serve as a mentor (well, of course, that's why agony uncle will be an ideal career for me). I was a bit worried when it also said that a Piscean is very particular and might have difficulty finding true love (time to write to Milly again, I feel).

Karen, I could hardly believe the next line – it said that if you are born on the 6th of March, you like to indulge your love of fine food and might be quite the epicure. Can you believe it? That's me all over. A word of caution to me, though, as it said that this is relatively harmless unless I resist daily exercise. I have to admit I did drag my paws going up the hill this morning. I wanted to stay home to help with the gardening instead – so many bushes to trim back and chew.

The website also described me as daring, unafraid to take chances and unlikely to fail because of my positive outlook. These are all attributes that I recognise in myself, so I'm totally converted to astrology and it has given me renewed confidence (not that I was lacking any) to forge forward with my career and activism.

You should check out your own star sign, Karen, to see if it is equally accurate.

Lots of love,

Coco x

Letter from Coco to Milly, Nairn

28th October 2022

Dearest, darling Milly,

Please forgive me for not being in touch sooner. I had a little medical issue that had to be sorted out – nothing important – so I wasn't able to write for a while. Anyway, you'll be pleased to hear that I'm now back on cloud nine. Life would be perfect were it not that you are in Nairn and I am in Perthshire.

You may be interested to know that I've been consulting my horoscope a lot recently, as I find it very encouraging. I hope you don't mind, but I took a look at yours, too, as I know that you were born under the sign of Aries. That means you are kind-hearted and daring, with the potential to do a great deal of good in the world. Isn't that wonderful? It says you display care and compassion, which I fully agree with.

One bit I found slightly worrying though was that for Aries individuals, there is apparently a thin line between love and friendship. Friends may become lovers and lovers may become friends. May I dare to hope that I am not on the friendship side of the line?

One characteristic that I agree suits you down to the ground is that Aries radiate energy and high spirits. After all my time with you, I can fully concur with that. Are you still drinking the camomile tea regularly, as I suggested?

In case you might be worried about our compatibility, what with you being a little spaniel born under the sign of Aries, and me being a large retriever born under the sign of Pisces, I decided to also see what the stars have to say about that. Well, I'm so glad I checked. A reliable source says we are both passionate romantic partners, well known for jumping deeply into romantic opportunities and being engrossed in the intensity and thrill of new love. I blush to tell you that it also says that Pisceans are extremely amorous and will go out of their way to do considerate things for their lover. I like to think that describes me very accurately.

Dearest Milly, I am so looking forward to seeing you again. It's written in the stars that we could have a wonderful relationship, so I believe we are quite literally a match made in heaven.

Lots of love,

Coco xxxxxxxxxxxxxx

Message from Coco to Karen

2nd November 2022

Dear Karen,

It was good of you to check out possible therapists for my housemates' separation anxiety problems, but there is no need to look any further as I have met the ideal person. His name is Hamish and he is my guru – what a relief to be working with him. He was recommended by a cockapoo friend, Jazz, who found him invaluable.

    Hamish and I are absolutely on the same wavelength. He's a retired gamekeeper who has worked alongside dogs all his life, so he completely understands what I'm going through. He and I have a strategy worked out to deal with the separation anxiety and disagreement over commands. He's going to demonstrate to my housemates how they should behave when they're on the lead so that they focus better on the sights and smells around, and don't just march forward, heads down, as though there are no interesting ditches, or sticks or bushes to be investigated. They get so little out of a walk, in comparison to me, that I wonder they bother going out at all.

He comes to the house a couple of times each week and he and I go off for a short walk together to discuss tactics and practise our moves. That's the easy bit. Then, we demonstrate our moves in the front garden while my housemates peer at us through the French windows. It's really quite heartbreaking to see their puzzled little faces looking out at us as we walk together, attached by the lead, perfectly synchronised. Because we understand each other so well, if Hamish decides to change direction or to stop and rest for a moment, I just go along with it. No tugging on the lead like my housemates do. Afterwards, Hamish has a word with them to tell them how they should behave and then goes home, but I have to take them through their paces and get them to do what Hamish did.

Oh, Karen, it is such hard work. They don't have a clue. While Hamish has a quiet authority and we work in harmony, these two have to be coaxed along all the time. Hamish says I just have to be patient and eventually they'll understand what I want them to do. I believe everything Hamish says; he's a real star.

Karen, how would you feel if I were to set up a Facebook page for all of the puppies, so that we could post photos of our housemates, tell each other stories of the crazy things they do and seek advice on problematic behaviour? Sometimes it's good to share worries – and I have plenty of those right now. I think I'll set one up anyway, if you could help me let everyone know.

And that's not my only source of worry. Ever since I read up on Milly's zodiac sign, I've been anxious that she may not commit to a long-term romantic relationship. She might actually be a bit flighty, so I'm wondering if I ought to revisit my idea of setting up a lonely hearts club and dating agency for puppies. If not for me, then for all the other puppies out there who are looking for love. I'll give it some thought and come back to you.

Love,

Coco x

PS Did you see in the news that Titan has been awarded a bravery medal for saving the lives of his housemates? Apparently, there was a house fire in the night and they were sound asleep in bed, so Titan had to race upstairs, bark as loudly as possible (good job he'd been practising), leap up onto the bed and jump up and down on top of them. Eventually, he managed to wake them up and lead them to safety. Isn't that incredible? Whoever thought that chihuahuas aren't brave? I'll bet people look up to him now, even if he is small.

Speaking of my correspondents, what do you think of the latest letter I've received and my draft reply? Should I be more sympathetic?

Letter to Coco from Precious Petal

30th October 2022

Dear Coco,

While I appreciate that this may not be the usual sort of problem on which you provide advice, it is one that is important to me, so I expect you to put everything else to one side and give it your full consideration. I am a five-year-old saluki with a gorgeous, flowing, honey-coloured coat, long silky ears and I can run like the wind. I am totally beyond compare; no other dog can match me for beauty and speed. I know you think golden retrievers are the bee's knees, but really? Have you ever met a saluki?

My problem is that while I yearn to have pups (I would make a wonderful mother and they would all be absolutely perfect and well behaved), I cannot find a male dog who is my equal. Obviously, I'm only interested in pure-bred salukis and there aren't many of them around. The few that I've been introduced to really weren't up to the mark. Most of them seemed friendly enough – overfriendly in one case – but I don't want my genes mixing with anything short of perfection. What if the pups turned out to look like their father rather than like me? *Quelle horreur!*

My maternal instincts are very strong and I am in my prime, but I can hear my biological clock ticking. Please do not suggest that I should lower my standards; surely it's not too much to ask for a perfect male specimen, who is my match in intelligence and looks. And whatever you do, do not suggest meeting up with some of your golden retriever pals; they're really not my type.

So, chop-chop, get to it and come up with proper advice. It can't be every day that a beauty like me comes knocking on your door.

Precious Petal

Draft Reply from Coco to Precious Petal

2nd November 2022

Dear Precious Petal (is that really your name?),

It's true that I have never received a letter quite like yours before. I would go so far as to say that I hope never to receive one again.

May I remind you that I act as an agony uncle out of the goodness of my heart and I do not get paid for it, by you or anyone else, so you can just drop that imperious tone with me. Has it occurred to you that the difficulty you are having in finding a mate may be because there are no male Salukis who would be prepared to hitch up with such a diva as you? It seems to me that when male salukis have tried to be friendly, you have acted haughtily and snubbed them. You say you have very high standards. Well, maybe they do, too, and they don't want an arrogant, self-centred, spoilt princess as mother to their pups.

Your best chance is to get cloned – after all, humans could do it for Dolly the Sheep, so I'm sure a saluki would be no problem. The trouble is that then there would be more salukis like you in the world.

Regards,

Coco

PS I would thank you not to disrespect golden retrievers – we may not run as fast as you, but we are much friendlier.

Message from Coco to Karen

8th November 2022

Dear Karen,

Thank you for your sound advice, as usual. I agree that I was uncharacteristically harsh and I've had another go at drafting a letter to Precious Petal, in which I bear in mind your concern that my reply is not just for her, but for any female dog who finds herself in PP's situation (do you think Precious Petal realises what her initials sound like? She might change her name if she did). And you are, of course, right that an intemperate reply such as the one I drafted isn't going to look too good when I send my portfolio to doggie magazines as part of my application to become an agony uncle. So, see what you think about my latest attempt, attached.

Some good news has just arrived, which I am over the moon about. I am to be awarded two weeks of respite from caring for my housemates. As you can imagine, looking after two needy adults is a full-time job – very taxing, both physically and mentally. All those walks I have to do, providing cuddles on demand, getting them up every morning and making sure they're not left on their own for too long – well, it's finally taken its toll and I'm absolutely frazzled (perhaps that's why I was so short with PP).

So, at the end of the month, I'm off to an exclusive country house for two whole weeks, where I'm fully expecting that my health and spirits can be restored in time for the festive season (my very first). I'm not sure what will happen with my housemates. I believe they are being sent somewhere they will be fully looked after while I have a much-needed break from my duties.

Reluctantly, I have to agree that you are also right about setting up a Facebook page. I really don't have the time to do it, what with everything else I'm involved in. I'll just share my stories when I next see all my brothers and sisters.

Love,

Coco x

Revised Letter from Coco to Precious Petal

8th November 2022

Dear Precious Petal (what an unusual name),

I apologise for the slight delay in replying to you, but I wanted to give your letter some serious consideration and also to consult on it with a dear friend who often advises me on the trickier correspondence I receive.

I understand your wish not to lower your standards, but I wonder if I can persuade you to *change* your standards. At present, you appear to have only two criteria: looks and intelligence, which you say you have in abundance. I'm sure these characteristics will be passed on to any pups you may have.

However, there are other criteria that you might like to consider. Wouldn't it be wonderful if your pups were happy little souls – friendly, sociable, loving and contented with their lives, enabling them to find housemates and friends who would be constant companions?

Precious Petal, I can't help feeling, from what lies

unsaid in your letter, that these characteristics are not ones with which you are blessed. I don't want to upset you, but perhaps you don't have many friends and you rely on your good looks to draw others to you. What you should be looking for in your pups is a combination of your looks and intelligence, along with a father's friendliness and loving nature. Of course, we cannot guarantee that that will be how it works out – we may find one or more of the pups inherits their father's looks and intelligence and your social skills, but is that not a risk worth taking? If you are going to be the excellent mother you describe, then you will love them all, not just those who are perfect (few of us are, sadly. Something for you to reflect on, perhaps).

So, how about re-engaging with some of those salukis you were introduced to before and assessing them in a different light, using friendliness and sociability as your criteria. You may find that amongst them is the perfect father for your pups. Do let me know how you get on and if you are in need of a godfather for your brood, I would be delighted to play the part.

Sincerely,

Coco

Message from Coco to Karen

18th November 2022

Dear Karen,

I really don't want my correspondence with you to decline into talk about the weather, but I just want to say that I am totally and utterly fed up with this constant rain. I expect it's the same in Fife as it has been here in Perthshire. My walks are curtailed, I get soaking wet, I have to be towelled dry (which I secretly enjoy) and then I'm not allowed on the carpets until I can guarantee that I won't leave a wet patch. And all this at least three times each day. What's to be done?

    Well, I'm pleased to say I have found a solution. One of my housemates has a little red car and she puts the back seats down when I travel with her. There are a couple of nice soft blankets in there and also a fluffy towel, so I have adopted it as my outdoor kennel. I get her to leave the boot open so that when I come back from a walk, I just hop in there (well, in fact, I still use the retractable steps, as hopping isn't in my repertoire of moves yet), lie on the towel while I lick myself dry and then curl up on the blankets.

I can happily spend most of the morning there sheltered from the incessant rain, passing the time with any visiting delivery men and the postie. They all know me now and call out, "Morning, Coco," and I give them a nod in reply and a wag of the tail. I feel I'm on my own little Noah's Ark in the middle of the deluge.

This arrangement works perfectly because as the car is parked in front of the house, I can also keep an eye on my housemates – they can't leave without me knowing, so I don't have to worry about them wandering off unaccompanied. I might write to Milly and suggest that she does the same. On second thoughts, I don't think lying still for two to three hours snoozing and contemplating the meaning of life is something that she could consider.

In the hope of sunnier days soon.

Love,

Coco x

Message from Coco to Karen

25th November 2022

Dear Karen,

I've become concerned recently about the nicknames I'm getting, which I feel don't reflect the serious side of my nature and can be a bit disrespectful. My housemates and some of their relatives have taken to calling me 'Coco Pops', 'Coca-Cola', 'Coco the Clown', 'Coconuts' and even 'Cocochino'. These are all rather ridiculous names and give a misleading image of me as someone who need not be taken seriously.

    So, I've been wondering about changing my name, but keeping the same initial. What would you think of 'Cornelius', say, or 'Conrad' or 'Cedric'? All of these have the necessary gravitas, I feel. Even 'Constantine' would be suitable, if a bit long, because it would remind people of 'Constantine the Great', who was a victorious Roman emperor I read about on Poodle. Much more in keeping with what I have in mind. Do let me know which of these you think would be best.

I'm pleased to report that I've almost finished my Christmas shopping. I'm all clued up about the festivities to come in a month's time, thanks to the source of endless information that is Poodle, and I thought I had better start early because of the time I'll be away at my country retreat receiving respite care. Naturally, my first thought was what to get Milly and so I was very pleased when out shopping with my housemates the other day to find a lovely soft toy called 'Kevin the Carrot'. Kevin is orange (as you would expect) and wears a kilt. I've checked under the kilt and there is nothing there to alarm an impressionable young female spaniel. I'm so looking forward to seeing Milly's expression when she unwraps it – do you think she'll let me play with it, too?

I want to give all my friends something to remind them of me, and so I've had some key rings made that have a photo of me on them. I look particularly wise and serene in this photo, so I'm rather pleased with them, particularly as they were quite cheap. As you know, I'm often a bit short of dosh.

All that was left then was to think of something for my housemates and I had to puzzle over this for quite some time. Eventually, I came up with a cracker of an idea – a buggy that attaches to the back of a bike, so that I can accompany them on cycle rides and not get left behind at home. I went for top-of-the-range with a luxurious padded seat, even though it cleaned me out, as I'm only prepared to travel in style. If you come up to Perthshire, you might see me whizzing through the countryside while one of my housemates does all the pedalling – an ideal arrangement, really.

So, roll on Christmas. I can't wait. What will Santa have for me?

Love,

Coco x

PS Wonderful news. I've just heard that Milly and I are definitely going to be spending Christmas together. I think there are still some energy drinks in the cupboard; better check.

PPS I meant to tell you, we have a new neighbour. She is a little black cocker spaniel called Pippa. I haven't met her yet, but I've been told that she's rather shy and nervous, so I want to be particularly welcoming. I really want her to like me. Perhaps I shouldn't be too boisterous around her.

Urgent Message from Coco to Karen

Later on 25th November 2022

Dear Karen,

Whatever you do, DO NOT READ the fourth paragraph of my earlier message. Please obliterate it. UNDER NO CIRCUMSTANCES BE TEMPTED TO READ IT.

I hope I caught you in time. If not, I didn't mean the bit about the present being cheap. It was *very, very* expensive.

In haste,

Coco x

Message from Coco to Karen

11th December 2022

Dear Karen,

I feel like a new dog! My respite was wonderful and I could have stayed for longer if only I didn't have to get back home for my housemates.

I had four personal attendants, two younger ones and two older ones. One was responsible for looking after my dietary requirements; one focused on my personal grooming; another made sure that I took adequate exercise, but didn't overdo it; and, finally, one was responsible for *fun*. I was the only client in residence, so I enjoyed being the centre of attention. Naturally, I expressed my gratitude in the usual way with lots of cuddles.

Now I'm back home and so are my housemates. I'm not sure where they went to while I was having respite. I think it was some sort of bootcamp where they would be licked into shape. Before they left I heard them refer to the *QM2*, which I think stands for the Queen's Military Establishment No.2, and how they wouldn't be able to leave for the duration of their stay. I hope they weren't treated too harshly; actually, I was a bit surprised to notice that they both looked a bit plumper and more relaxed when they returned, so it must have been a very easy regime.

Anyway we've settled back into our routine. I'm loving this cold, frosty weather and regularly race around like mad in the front garden. I can't wait for the first snow to come – I've never seen any before and I can't imagine what it will be like, but my housemates say it's tremendous fun.

I'm a bit disappointed that you didn't like my idea about changing my name, but I can understand your reasoning. I've been Coco for nine months and everyone knows me as that. And OK, the nicknames are just a way for people to show their affection for me, so I shouldn't really complain. I'll stick with Coco and will work harder at acquiring an air of gravitas.

Love,

Coco x

Message from Coco to Karen

17th December 2022

Dear Karen,

When I woke up this morning, there was snow – heaps and heaps of it, all over the garden. And the housemates are right for once – it is tremendous fun! I can't believe how wonderful it is. I've been rolling in it, sliding through it and having snowball fights with my housemates. They throw snowballs at me and I try to catch them. It's jolly difficult. My winter coat is keeping me lovely and warm, but they have to be covered in layers and layers of human fur, which I believe is called *clothing*.

That reminds me of something I was going to ask you, Karen. Do you think I'm an impatient sort of a guy? No, I don't think so either, but I do get terribly frustrated every morning. You see, when I wake up, I find that I just need a big stretch, a couple of gigantic yawns, a really good shake and then I'm ready for all the challenges of the day ahead. But you wouldn't believe the rigmarole that my housemates go through.

Well, first of all, they seem to think that it's necessary to get into a rain machine every morning. They call it a shower, which I think is to do with rain, so I've worked out for myself what it is. Perhaps Poodle could give me a job.

Why, when they're so opposed to going outside in the rain, do they have a shower machine in their house? They say it's so they can wash, but that's just silly. I find that a few good licks of my nether regions is quite sufficient, along with the occasional lick of my paws.

Then, there is the endless routine of the male housemate shaving off what little natural fur he has – I tremble at the thought – and the female housemate applying all sorts of different lotions to various parts of her body. They say it's to enhance their appearance, but I don't understand the need for it at all – I have whiskers that I think are rather fetching and a brisk brush of the coat is surely better than all this moisturising and shaving nonsense.

And why do they have to brush their teeth so often? Is there something wrong with them? I never brush my teeth and the vet says that they are in excellent condition, so it just goes to show you that it's totally unnecessary.

But it doesn't stop there, because then they have to decide what to wear and they dither about putting on one thing and then another. It's beyond me why the male housemate shaves off his fur, only to put artificial fur on. I have the one winter coat and it does me all year round. Very handy. The whole thing is such a palaver that I have usually gone back to sleep by the time they're ready. And let's face it, despite the daily routine, neither of them is going to make it to the front cover of *Vogue*, are they?

Now that it's winter, things have got even worse. One

of them will ask me if I want to go for a walk, but before we can even get out the door, they have to put on extra layers of clothes, boots and gloves. And then, if they think it will be icy, they put studs on their boots to stop them slipping.

What is the matter? I have four paws, with no studs or treads, and I can skip and frolic in the snow without losing my balance. I really don't know what is wrong with the pair of them.

When we eventually leave the house, one of them will inevitably realise that they've left their hat behind or forgotten my treats. It's a miracle I get any exercise at all. Fortunately, if I'm ready before them, which I usually am, and the person who feeds Mick and Coco is in the field next door, I can run round there and he shares the packet of peppermints he brings for the horses with me. Ooh, I love them. I never get sweeties at home.

So, no, I don't think I'm impatient, I just have limits to my tolerance and those two test it every day. But I'm staying chilled.

Love,

Coco x

PS I've just received a heart-warming letter from Buddy. His best friend is back from university for the Christmas holidays and has put loads of presents for Buddy under the Christmas tree. So has his little sister. The three of them are sticking together like glue for the whole holiday period and Buddy has come to accept that that is how it's going to be for the next few years.

Message from Coco to Karen

27th December 2022

Dear Karen,

Oh, Karen, I had a wonderful Christmas – three whole days with Milly and some of my favourite humans. Milly seemed to like Kevin the Carrot – as did I, so it's just as well I bought one for myself too. Her present to me was a furry green monster. I hope she doesn't ask me about it next time we see each other as I've already pulled all the stuffing out of it, so it's looking a bit limp now.

Everyone liked the (very expensive) key rings that I'd had made with my photo on them; I hope you liked yours, too. The Christmas tree was lovely with all sorts of baubles and stars on it. Milly and I had fun taking the baubles off it and running away with them.

One big disappointment, though, was that my housemates didn't like the idea of the luxury cycling buggy and it's been sent back. Apparently, towing me round the countryside while I lounge in comfort is not something they're prepared to entertain. They really are no fun at all.

Because it was Christmas, I was allowed some tasty treats with my meals even though I'm supposed to be watching my weight. Well, I am watching it, it's just not going anywhere. But even though it was Christmas, I still wasn't allowed on the furniture. Normally, it doesn't bother me, but Milly was lying on the couch all the time, looking down at me, and I got told off by my housemate for going up to join her. I believe this is discriminatory and possibly sexist and size-ist. Milly looked so comfortable snuggled up with a cushion. I would love to have snuggled up with her.

But I did get a chance for a romantic interlude with Milly. When our housemates were playing *Feliz Navidad* on the music system, she and I slipped into the next room and did some boogying together. She showed me some really good moves, very alluring, and though I say it myself, I was pretty groovy.

Now the housemates and I are home again and although we weren't away for long, wildlife seems to have taken over the garden, so I'm on full-time alert. I've been trying to eradicate moles by digging into their molehills and barking at them. A friend has told me that I need to be careful, though, as they might bite me on the nose – so I bark at them from a distance. Then there are squirrels to be chased and all manner of birds. It's a full-time job. Even when we're out on walks, I have to keep a lookout for deer and chase them up into the woods so that they're not on my patch. It's no wonder I have the physique of an athlete, given all the running around that I do.

Roll on 2023. I can't imagine what adventures are in store.

Love,

Coco x

Message from Coco to Karen

1st January 2023

Dear Karen,

Happy New Year and best wishes for 2023.

I'm writing this from Edinburgh, where we are spending a few days. I was pleased about that as I thought it meant I would be able to celebrate Hogmanay and stay up for the fireworks at the castle, which are supposed to be splendid, despite the noise. Unfortunately, I decided to take a nap beforehand and slept through it all. My housemates tell me the fireworks were really, *really* loud and the glass was rattling in the windowpanes, but I can't say I heard anything.

It's rather nice being back in the city and I've met up with a few of my friends here. I went out for a walk yesterday and I saw a small terrier in her front garden, standing in a basin of soapy water while her housemate washed her. I quickly walked on and tried to divert my housemates' attention by chasing a plastic wrapper. I don't want them to get any ideas about bathing me. The indignity!

I'm attaching the latest letter I've been sent by a French bulldog called Maurice, along with my draft reply. You'll see why I'm being careful when you read it.

So, it's 2023 and yesterday my housemates and I all sat down to write our New Year's resolutions. They didn't come up with anything very challenging – just losing some weight, taking more exercise… blah, blah, blah. I wanted mine to be more life-changing, so I chose four and I'm determined to achieve them:

1. Earn an income. It's essential that I either start my own company or get a paid job. Without a steady income, how can I become the pillar of society that I wish to be? I've drafted a letter to send out to the editor of *Pup World*. Let me know what you think of it.
2. Have a tattoo of the word 'Milly' on my chest, where my heart is – but not to the accompaniment of fireworks, as is the preference of those getting inked in Edinburgh. Even without the bangs and crashes, though, this might be a bit painful, but it is an expression of my love for her so must be endured. The only problem is that the tattooist will need to shave my chest to do it, then all the hair will grow back again and no one (i.e. Milly) will be able to see the tattoo. Have you any suggestions of how to overcome this problem?
3. I plan for 2023 to be the year I get engaged to Milly. I want our relationship to be formalised and long-term, so I have to choose the right time and place to pop the question. Perhaps at the end of a candlelit dinner for two.
4. Finally, in case Milly turns me down, I am resolved to dig the most enormous hole in the garden, reach

Australia and become a jackeroo. I know you're going to tell me it will be too hot for me down under, but perhaps I could just go during the Australian winter and then come back to Scotland for our winter. (How strange that their year is back to front, but snow in June does appeal. Does it snow in Australia? That'll be my next Poodle search.) That way, I would avoid all summer weather, which would be a great relief.

I do have a subsidiary list of less-important resolutions, like learning to swim; finding a way of getting through the fence in the back garden, so that I can visit Mick and Coco's field and get peppermints more often; training my housemates to walk off the lead so that I can have more time running free; and so on. But the first four are my main goals and I'll be starting to plan them straightaway.
Wish me luck.

Love,

Coco x

Message from Maurice to Coco
28th December 2022

Yo Coco, how's it hanging?

Maurice here – I'm a French bulldog, so cool you'd think I'd just popped out of the freezer. You seem like an upright sort of a dude – probably not someone I would normally hang out with, but I'm hoping you might be able to offer some advice.

    I run with a gang – in fact, I'm the main dog. No dispute; everyone has to do as I say or I'll be dishing out Trouble with a capital T. There are four of us all living in the same street: Spud at number eleven is a Staffordshire bull terrier; Buster at number eighteen is a boxer; and Knuckles at number twenty-one is of indeterminate origin, but as fierce as they come. Knuckles' real name is actually Benjy, but don't ever call him that unless you want a shedload of aggro.

    We control the street. This means intimidating all other dogs, especially the chicks; tormenting cats; barking at passers-by and generally making a nuisance of ourselves with the postie and delivery men. Wherever the rubber hits the road, that's where you'll find us. Although I'm a tough nut, I have to be constantly watching my back so that I can defend my role as leader. Knuckles, especially, is always trying to overthrow me.

It's important to maintain my macho exterior at all costs, even though when I'm at home with my housemates, I'm a complete pushover. Giving off the right kind of smell is part of the deal, so at every opportunity I roll in something particularly putrid. This might include a dead fish if we've been to the beach, deer poo if we've been into the countryside or just raking through people's bins if they've got overturned in a high wind. And that's how I like to smell – high! It confirms my position as a badass not to be meddled with.

"So, what's your problem?" you might ask. Well, it's my housemates. It used to be that when I rolled in something really smelly, they would turn the garden hose on me. Fortunately, that didn't get it all off and so I was still able to strut my stuff with an odour hanging around me. But my housemates have now gone and bought some perfumed soap to rub into my coat, which not only obliterates the pong, but also leaves me smelling of lavender and roses.

This has completely destroyed my street cred and Spud, Buster and Knuckles are mocking me. They say, "Ooh la la! Here comes a French poodle with his eau de cologne. Next thing we know, he'll be wearing ribbons round his neck instead of a collar and a diamanté clasp on his head."

What am I to do, Coco? I've got territory to control and I need mates alongside me to do that. I can't skulk at home all day waiting for the perfume to fade. So, turn your colossal brain and sharp intellect to my problem, please, even though it's a bit outside of your own personal experience.

Gotta bounce now,

Maurice

Draft Letter from Coco to Maurice

30th December 2022

Dear Maurice,

Well, you may think you are one cool customer, but let me tell you, you are a delinquent and so are your so-called friends. If you don't stop your antisocial behaviour pdq, then you are all likely to find yourselves in the dog pound. I know you won't want to hear this, but the path you are going down can lead to only one destination – the slammer. Four young lives wasted!

Maurice, are you really a leader? If you are, then show me. Get Spud, Buster and Knuckles to follow you down a different path – one where you become an asset to your community, not a source of worry and fear. Personally, I don't think you can do it because, while you believe you are top dog, you are really just a slave to your testosterone, being manipulated by your 'friends' into increasingly awful behaviour.

So, show me what you can do. Yes, you could be a leader in the canine community, but I don't think you've got the guts. Prove me wrong if you dare. And have you not got any brains? The easy answer to your dilemma is: stop rolling in smelly stuff. Then your housemates won't have to bathe you. If your position as leader depends on how you smell, then you're on pretty thin ice.

I'll wait to hear from you, 'big guy'.

Coco

Letter to Editor of Pup World

1st January 2023

Dear Ed,

May I introduce myself? My name is Coco and I am a ten-month-old golden retriever with a great deal of life experience behind me. I am known for being sympathetic to the woes of others and for always lending an ear – two, in fact, and very soft, velvety ones they are – to those in need of sound advice on life's challenges.

As a result, I regularly receive letters from other puppies and dogs who find themselves in difficulty, often with their housemates, and need to know the best thing to do to resolve their situation. Drawing on my vast experience and wealth of empathy, I am able to guide them in the right direction and have evidence that my advice often leads to positive results.

I notice that your esteemed magazine does not have an agony page, so I would like to put myself forwards as an agony uncle, providing several column inches each week. You see, the advice I give to my correspondents would be of benefit to dogs and puppies throughout the country and would enhance the reputation of your magazine hugely. It would give you a competitive edge, increase your circulation and render other doggie magazines impotent.

I have an extensive portfolio of case studies, which I would be happy to show you. These include letters from dogs who fear losing the housemates they adore, dogs who suffer from breed dysphoria, others who are seeking love and companionship, one who hears her biological clock ticking and another whom I believe I have been able to pull back from the verge of delinquency. These are all issues in which your readers may be able to see parallels in their own lives.

If you are interested, we can discuss terms. While I live quite modestly, I am saving up for a motorbike and sidecar so that I can visit my sweetheart and take her out for a spin in the countryside, stopping off for slap-up lunches at our favourite watering holes. So, reasonably generous remuneration for my services will be required.

I look forward to hearing from you.

Yours sincerely,

Coco Canine Esquire

Message from Coco to Karen

3rd January 2023

My dearest Karen,

I want you to know that you have been the best friend any puppy could ask for. It has been a privilege to know you. I say this now because this will be the last letter you receive from me.

You see, I'm dying and I need to let you know how much you mean to me before I shuffle off this mortal coil and head for the great unknown. I am lying here in my basket very, very unwell. I've been sick all over the sitting room carpet and, unfortunately, I'm suffering from acute diarrhoea as well. Bit embarrassing, really, as we're still in Edinburgh, where it's a task and a half for a puppy to get any privacy. However, embarrassment is the least of my concerns.

Could it be dysentery or some sort of amoebic infestation? Or could it be the rotting vegetable I found in the front garden yesterday and quickly ate before my housemate could take it off me? Whatever it is, I fear I will not survive.

I feel constantly nauseous and my gut is spasming and doing contortions. I haven't eaten for the last twenty-four hours even when chicken and cheese have been offered, so I know the situation is serious. My housemates are whispering in low funereal tones, saying things like, "Do you think he'll make it?" They're talking about my chances of survival rather than whether I'll reach the garden before my next attack of the squitters.

Given the gravity of the situation, I feel I have to put my affairs in order and choose the music for my funeral. I've left all my worldly goods to Milly – my bed, blankets, towels, bowls and all my toys except for the brown bear whose face I've chewed off and the green dragon that I gutted. I've left these to my housemates to remember me by.

I humbly request that my ashes be scattered on Nairn beach, where I have spent some of my happiest times with Milly. Oh, Karen, how I now regret that rotting vegetable as I lie here at death's door. For the opening number at my funeral, I've chosen 'Little Doggie'. I know that it's more of a Christmas song than a hymn, but it sums up the burdens I have carried while I've tried to do some good in the world.

And then, at the end, when everyone is leaving the chapel, I thought a rousing rendering of 'Good-bye-ee!' might lighten the mood. Although there is a danger that it will be drowned out by the wailing of the bereaved.

I shall write to Milly to say farewell. She must be brave and hopefully she will one day find another beau almost as caring and handsome as me. Oh, that will be a difficult letter to write.

Oh, oh, another spasm in my gut… I think I'd better…

Letter from Coco to Milly, Nairn

3rd January 2023

My dearest, darling Milly,

Please lie down while you are reading this, in case you fall into a faint and do yourself some damage. I have tragic news to impart.

It seems that my life is about to be cut short; my number's up; I have been felled in my prime. Some ghastly disease has taken over my body and I doubt that I will still be alive when this letter reaches you. You have been the love of my life; there has only ever been you in my heart. Please send an obituary to *The Times* and remember to include mention of my bravery and exceptional good looks.

My final words of advice to you, so you may lead a long and happy life without me, are 'Be sure not to eat any rotting vegetables that you find in the front garden'.

Adieu, my love,

Coco xxx

Message from Coco to Karen

5th January 2023

Dear Karen,

Sorry I couldn't finish that last letter, but no matter because the panic's over. Cheer up – I'm alive and well and feeling on top form! In fact, my brush with death has made me realise how wonderful life is and how I must not waste a minute in idle pastimes. *Carpe diem* will be my new motto.

 I'm sorry to have given everyone a scare, but it seems that the grim reaper is not calling on me just yet. Some medication from the vet here in Edinburgh has settled my tummy, the sickness is over, my gut is back to normal and I'm enjoying my food again. Phew, that was a close call. My housemates say that I was unnecessarily melodramatic and they carried on being cheery – were they ignorant of the fact that I was about to pop my clogs?

 To celebrate my return to the land of the living, my housemates have said that they've got a surprise for me, but won't tell me what it is. I'm rather excited – I don't know what it can be. A visit to Disneyland, perhaps, to meet Pluto? A trip to Nairn to see Milly and reassure her that I am fully recovered? Another few days of pampering at my country retreat? Who knows? I'll send you another message as soon as I find out.

I meant to say thank you for the advice about digging to Australia if Milly spurns my offer of marriage. I'd forgotten about the dingoes. Poodle tells me they have a reputation for being rather unfriendly and they run in packs. If they were to pick on me, I don't think I'd have much of a chance. I've never really been a scrapper, being too urbane and sophisticated. So we'll just have to hope that Milly doesn't turn me down, won't we?

You're probably right that having the word 'Milly' tattooed on my chest is a bit of a waste of time and money if no one sees it. Perhaps a little charm on my collar that says 'I love Milly' would be better, after all, and she would be able to see that. I'll get on to it straightaway.

Love,

Coco x

PS I hope you didn't go out and buy any new black clothes for my funeral. I'd hate to think I'd put you to unnecessary expense. Perhaps you could return them and get a refund.

Message from Coco to Karen

8th January 2023

Dear Karen,

I'm back home in Perthshire again, having left the big city behind. But before we departed, I persuaded my housemates that we should act like tourists for an afternoon and visit some of our favourite places. First stop was obviously Greyfriars Bobby. I wanted to pay my respects to this loyal Skye terrier. Imagine being so famous that you get a bronze statue made in your memory and over 220,000 people come to visit it every year. Wow!

Since we were in that part of town, our next stop was Edinburgh Castle. I know everyone generally goes there to see Mons Meg and all the battlements and the lovely view across Edinburgh to the Firth of Forth, but I had a different reason for going. I wanted to visit the little garden where the brave dogs who fought alongside soldiers are buried.

We weren't allowed into the garden, but we could see from the battlements above the graves of over twenty dogs. Yum Yum, Tim and Dobbler travelled with the Argyll and

Sutherland Highlanders to China, Sri Lanka and South Africa while Jess fought with the Black Watch. Khan, a German shepherd, is also buried there. He volunteered as a rifleman during WWII with his best friend Lance Corporal Jimmy Muldoon. When they were overcome by German forces during the Battle of the Scheldt in northern Belgium and had to swim for their lives, Khan saved Jimmy by dragging him to shore when the weight of his kit became too heavy for him in the muddy waters.

Oh, I get a lump in my throat just thinking about it. What a brave dog. He was awarded a medal for his courage and I'm pleased to say that he and his friend both survived the war. It's a lovely little cemetery, where all these brave dogs can rest in peace.

After the castle, we wandered down to Princes Street Gardens to see the statue of a deerhound called Maida, whose housemate was Sir Walter Scott (he is also part of the statue, albeit a minor detail). No doubt her calming presence helped him a lot with his writing.

Also in the gardens, we came across the statue of Bum, a dog from San Diego. I don't really know why he has a statue all to himself as, apparently, he was very disreputable, going around picking fights, cadging food and even drinking alcohol. During a fight with a bulldog, he was hit by a train and lost half his right foreleg. It's a bit of a mystery why the people of San Diego gifted a monument of such a reprobate to Edinburgh.

After a lovely afternoon, we all got an ice cream and walked the rest of the way to our accommodation. It's nice to do things in the city that I can't do at home in Perthshire.

We arrived home to good news, Karen! There was a letter waiting for me from the editor of *Pup World*, offering me a three-month probationary trial as Agony Uncle. How about that? My journalistic career starts here. The downside is that it's an unpaid probationary period, but think of the experience. You can't put a price on that.

Love,

Coco x

Message to Karen

15th January 2023

Dear Karen,

Don't you find these long winter evenings are beginning to drag? I've now discovered what the housemates meant about the nights drawing in during the autumn – they get longer. Why you humans can't just say what you mean, I will never know.

    I keep hoping that spring is on its way, but instead, we just have more snow and ice, so I decided to devise some constructive way to fill my evenings. After all, I have to stick to my new *carpe diem* motto. The idea I came up with is rather whizzo and a good investment for the future.

    I've enrolled for an online vocational training course in guarding. Although I don't plan on following that as a profession, I still think it will be handy for my housemates to have a highly skilled and dedicated guard on the premises to see off any unwelcome intruders. I'm going to have to work very hard to complete the course successfully and get my Level 1 diploma.

One of my housemates has offered to mentor me, but what she knows about security is anyone's guess. She left the front door unlocked the whole time I was away for my respite. We're fortunate that we didn't come home to an empty house, ransacked by burglars. However, I'm humouring her by pretending that she's a great help.

There are three modules to work on at Level 1: barking, growling and identifying suspicious characters. I'm making some progress on all three, but barking is probably the one with which I'm having most success. I've developed a lovely deep bark, which is the first step, but I've not yet got the hang of when I should use it. Today, I barked loudly at one of my housemates when he came back from the shops, but apparently that's not appropriate; I'm supposed to wag my tail in those circumstances. It's all very confusing.

I'm not so good at growling because I only ever use it when we're playing tug of war and I'm pretending to be fierce. No one has ever looked the slightest bit scared when I've done it, so I need to practise that a lot more. I thought I was doing OK at identifying suspicious characters when I saw someone lurking by the fence, looking as though they were hiding in the trees, and I barked very loudly to alert my housemates. In fact, it was only Mary next door pruning her rose bushes.

So, it's still a work in progress, but I hope to have completed the course by the spring when the longer days come again. Then, next winter, I can maybe progress to Level 2: snarling and pinning intruders to the ground. I'm rather looking forward to that and hoping that my housemates will let me practise on them.

Thanks for reading over my reply to Maurice. I'm very glad that you agree with the stern tone I have adopted. It was rather unlike me and I do hope he doesn't come round to my house with his gang to beat me up. For the sake of society, I had to stand firm and call him out for the hooligan that he is.

Love,

Coco x

Message from Coco to Karen

23rd January 2023

Dear Karen,

Remember I told you that my housemates had a surprise in store for me? Well, they gave it to me yesterday – it was an afternoon outing with three of my sisters and it was super-duper wonderful. We all visited Beecraigs Park together and went wild.

These girls are something else, I can tell you! They got up to all sorts. To prevent one of us getting the blame for anything naughty that we did, we made a pact at the beginning of the afternoon that whatever one did, the others all had to follow. So, when Harley jumped into the muddiest, blackest, deepest ditch and the other two sisters followed, what could I do? I had to leap in after them.

We heard the collective groan from all the housemates, but we didn't care. We just wallowed for a while, got out and then all gave ourselves a good shake – which is when the groans turned into shrieks, as we were quite close to the housemates at the time. Then, when the one called

Molly tore off into the woods and raced around in the undergrowth, ignoring calls for her to come back, the other two sisters followed and, of course, so did I. We only returned when one of the housemates got some sausage out of her pocket and called for us to come and get it.

But nobody was really angry because they could see that we were having such a good time. So good, in fact, that we're going to meet up again next month and perhaps two of my brothers will be there as well. Then, in March, it will be the big birthday party when you will have all twelve of your puppies back with you again. You must try not to get too emotional, Karen; it has to be a happy occasion.

Karen, I have some very good news to tell you. Precious Petal has been back in touch to let me know that she is now the proud mother of five adorable puppies. She says that she clicked with the friendly saluki, after all, and now they are parents. According to her, the puppies are perfect in every way and she wanted to thank me for my advice and encouragement. In fact, she's so grateful that she has called one of the boys 'Coco'. It's so nice when everything works out and there is a happy ending.

I haven't heard back from Maurice, but I've fast-tracked my guarding training so that I'm on full alert in case he finds out where I live.

Love,

Coco x

Message from Coco to Karen

26th January 2023

Dear Karen,

Did you have a good Burns Supper last night? We toasted the bard in traditional fashion and I played a full part in proceedings.

    We started off with one of my housemates addressing the haggis. He took a bit longer than I would have liked, as I was ravenous and the smell of the haggis, neeps and tatties was mouth-watering, but he eventually finished going on about it being a chieftain of the puddin' race and we all got down to demolishing it – in pretty short order, in my case. After that, my other housemate recited 'Tam o' Shanter', which had me on the edge of my seat, but I'm pleased to report that Meg got Tam over the bridge at the end and the witches didn't catch him. It was a close call, though, and a great relief to me.

    Then, after we'd eaten our cranachan pudding, it was my turn to perform and I recited Burns' *The Twa Dugs*. Well, it went down a storm, especially as I did actions with it. When I got to the bit 'His gawsie tail, wi' upward curl / Hung owre his hurdies wi' a swirl', I flicked my tail up and waved it about, almost bringing the house down. We were a very merry company – the only slight disappointment being that I wasn't allowed a nip with my haggis.

I was still enjoying the afterglow of a wonderful evening this morning when the postie arrived at full speed in his van and handed me a letter marked 'Urgent' in large red letters. Oh dear, Karen, Maurice has got himself into dreadful trouble – or 'bovver', as he would probably say. I'm attaching his letter and I am off now to try to compose some lines to go to the judge before the hearing on Monday. (I had to poodle some of the words Maurice used, and I discovered that rather than facing a large bird of prey, he meant a judge when he said 'beak'. He's worse than you humans for not saying what he means!) I need to be sufficiently convincing for Maurice to get a stay of execution – literally, if his colourful vernacular is to be believed. I only hope I can do it.

Any words of advice are very welcome.

Love,

Coco x

PS I went to see Charli in a trampolining competition on Saturday. She did really well. Perhaps not as well as if I'd actually been on the trampoline with her but good enough all the same. In fact I didn't see any other puppies there – probably another case of blatant discrimination.

Letter from Maurice to Coco

25th January 2023

Yo, Coco, my bro,

I hope you're feeling totally boomshakalaka. No worries, no worries, man. I've just got a small favour to ask and I'm thinking that being the totally square shooter you are, you won't mind helping me out.

The long and the short of it is that I've been stitched up and my guess is that Knuckles is to blame. It's all about a brief dust-up with the cat at number thirty-two. It was getting a bit uppity and I had to put it in its place. Some cats don't have tails anyway, so I don't know what all the sweat is about, just because it is now missing a couple of inches.

This all happened before your letter of advice, which I've been trying really hard to follow, landed on my doormat. But as I mentioned to you, Knuckles has been itching to overthrow me, so my guess is he snitched on me to the fuzz and the next thing I know the rozzers are at the door, I'm in cuffs, my housemates are pleading for leniency and I'm being driven to the pound with the full blues-and-twos.

I go in front of the beak on Monday and there seems to be little doubt that, with my record, he'll be reaching for the black cap and I'll be swinging before Friday. I'm defending myself as I couldn't find a lawyer who would do it. I'm only allowed to send one letter and I urgently need a character reference from an upstanding member of society. I immediately thought of you as you're the only decent guy who's ever bothered to try to help me.

Could you get that reference to me by Monday latest? I promise I am really trying to mend my ways. I feel so bad about kicking up dust for my housemates, who have always been kind to me, no matter how badly I behaved.

You're my only hope, Coco. I know you can slay them. Will you see your way to helping out a wrong 'un like me?

Hasta la vista, Coco. Over and out,

Maurice

Letter from Coco to Judge Hangem

27th January 2023

Your Honour,

I am writing with regard to prison inmate Maurice. He has approached me to provide him with a character reference prior to his appearance before you on Monday next. As you no doubt will be, I am appalled by his repeated antisocial behaviour and can understand that you will want to mete out the harshest of punishments. I have no intention of trying to defend what he has done.

What you may be unaware of is that Maurice got in touch with me, as a mentor of sorts, sometime after the incident with the unfortunate cat. I counselled him that his behaviour was entirely unacceptable and that he not only had to mend his ways, but he had to lead his friends along a different path and clean up the neighbourhood generally. He has assured me that he has started to follow my advice and the contretemps with the cat is a historic incident.

I believe that Maurice has leadership qualities that can be used for positive outcomes rather than for causing mayhem as he has done in the past. These are very valuable qualities which, if harnessed, could be used for the good of the community. May I therefore respectfully suggest that rather than incarcerate Maurice or, worse, eliminate him, you would consider putting his talents to good use to prevent further hooliganism.

I trust you will accept my suggestion as a constructive alternative and save a young life.

Yours sincerely,

Coco Canine Esquire

Message from Coco to Karen

31st January 2023

Dear Karen,

First, the good news – Maurice is no longer on death row. He has had a reprieve. As I requested, the judge showed leniency and Maurice has been sentenced to one hundred hours of community service in a home for stray cats and dogs. I think this will test him, but he is a lucky fellow.

Then, the bad news – the above sentence is on condition that I act as his guardian and am accountable for his behaviour. This is all because his housemates have shown themselves to be completely incompetent and allowed his behaviour to get totally out of hand. What a penalty I am paying for trying to help him. I don't see that I have any choice in the matter – if I refuse, then Maurice has a date with the hangman.

Oh, I've just had an awful thought – maybe, since he's of French origin, the executioner would guillotine him. *Sacré bleu!*

What would you do in my position, Karen? How can I ensure that he stays on the straight and narrow? And how do I keep him away from the pernicious influence of Spud, Buster and Knuckles?

I really don't need this extra responsibility at the moment when I am practically on starvation rations. I barely have any strength. Life is cruel – my housemates tuck into three square meals a day, supplemented by cake, biscuits and chocolate. They think I don't see them snacking, but I can smell the chocolate a mile off and I don't understand why I can't have any. They say it's bad for dogs, but let's face it, it's not exactly healthy for humans either.

While all this guzzling is going on, I have to subsist on two meals a day of the biscuity stuff. I hang around the kitchen a lot hoping for a few offcuts, but no joy. I have to admit, though, it is paying off. We went to see Jan the vet today and I have lost the required weight. Now I am even more perfect than I was before, even if I'm so weak I can barely raise a paw. She gave me a treat to get me onto the scales – which was a bit ironic, given that it's she who insists on this frugal diet.

I fear I am reduced to scavenging. We were up on the grouse moors yesterday and I found a dead rabbit, so I had a good crunch on that. And the other day, I found an equally dead bird and ate a bit of that, too. My housemates get mad at me, but needs must. I have to have more calories and if they come from meat, then so much the better.

Love from your slim, trim friend,

Coco x

Message from Coco to Karen

6th February 2023

Dear Karen,

Thank you so much for your advice on Maurice, you're absolutely right. The devil makes work for idle paws and he needs gainful employment to fill his time and to keep him on the straight and narrow. The community service is not going to be enough on its own.

    I think it would also help if he had a girlfriend who was supportive and could give him some personal hygiene advice, so I may have the perfect solution. With all my commitments, including an increasing number of letters from dogs in distress thanks to my profile having been raised by my weekly column in *Pup World*, I have not been able to move forwards on the idea of a canine dating agency and the government seems to be doing absolutely nothing about it. With Maurice's organisational and leadership qualities, he could be ideally placed to set this up – under my close supervision, of course. I'm going to get in touch with him about it straightaway.

Thank you for asking whether I had a nice weekend; in fact, it wasn't that great. Although it started off well with a day on the beach in St Andrews on Saturday, which I loved, it ended badly – my housemate and I went along to another training session at the local village hall on Sunday.

Really, Karen, I don't understand the point of putting six young dogs in a hall together and not expecting them to want to socialise with each other. Also, if the trainer is going to walk around with enormous quantities of treats in her pocket, then of course I'll want to be close beside her all the time in case some might come my way. My housemate and I had a constant tussle. We were both exhausted after a couple of hours and left early, so that we could come home and lie down in a dark room. Fortunately, I think that spells the death knell for training in this household.

I hope the arrangements for the first birthday party are coming along nicely. Less than four weeks to go.

Love,

Super-excited Coco x

Message from Coco to Karen

8th February 2023

Dear Karen,

Thank you for replying so promptly to my last message, but there is really no need to be alarmed about Maurice taking on the setting-up of the puppies' dating agency. He has learned his lesson and his brush with the law has given him the shock that he needed. His community service is going well, although it seems to have coincided with a steep decline in the number of cats and dogs coming to the home for refuge and a large number being rapidly rehoused. Never mind, I'm sure it's all valuable experience for him.

    Besides, as I said, regarding the dating agency, I shall supervise him closely. I've given him a number of potential clients to work on and he is putting their profiles onto the database and starting the matching process as I write. My most recent correspondent, whose message I attach, will be a challenging client for the agency. I'm sure he's a great fellow, but not necessarily every girl's idea of a good catch.

We had a lovely day at the beach again yesterday, except it could have ended badly. We took my absolute favourite ball with us (it squeaks and is a bit spikey), but my housemates kept throwing it into the sea like they didn't care about it. Each time they did it, I had to rush into the water to retrieve it, otherwise it could have been washed away and I would have had to go home without it.

I tried to hold on to it at all times, but when a treat was offered (beef-flavoured biscuits yesterday), I had to drop the ball in order to take the treat. Then, one of the housemates would snatch it up and throw it away into the sea again. I was back and forward, back and forward dozens of times. I don't know why they are so disrespectful of other people's possessions – it was extremely thoughtless of them.

Fortunately, I was very alert and they never actually threw the ball so far that I would have had to swim out of my depth to get it. I managed to return to the car with it at the end of the walk, so that was a big relief, even though I was completely exhausted and slept all the way home.

Love,

Coco x

Letter to Coco from Paddy

4th February 2023

Dear Coco,

Top o' the morning to you, boyo. My name's Paddy and I'm an Irish wolfhound – you know the type: large, grey, hairy, a bit dishevelled. It's true that I'm no dinger, but to be sure, I've got a heart of gold. Maybe I spend a bit too much time hanging out with my muckers, kicking a ball about, enjoying the craic, and making myself scarce whenever I hear the word 'walk' mentioned or the grooming brush comes out. Worst of all, I head for the hills if I see one of my housemates coming towards me with a toothbrush and paste. I like to take life easy and I don't see why it's necessary to get all smart and spruced up.

    Trouble is, you see, my muckers are all male and it would be just grand to have my own old doll to come home to every night and snuggle up with. But sure, I'm up to ninety every day what with making sure I see all my pals, scratching at the matted hair behind my ears and keeping a wary eye out in case anyone tries to get me to a grooming parlour.

I haven't had time to do any courting. The few lassies that I have approached seem to prefer to give me a wide berth. I don't know what their problem is. OK, so I'm a few kilos too heavy but, hey, I enjoy my food, I'm not keen on exercise and I think lots of lassies might find me quite cuddly.

Can you help? I need to find someone who can see behind the scraggy appearance and love me for what I am. No floozies, please. I'm looking for a real sweetie to make my muckers green.

Gotta hit the road now. My housemate will be back from work in 10 minutes. I just know she's gonna want to go for a walk so I'm off round to my pal's house where there's always sport on the telly and a comfy rug to watch it from.

Paddy

Draft Reply from Coco to Paddy

6th February 2023

Dear Paddy,

Thank you for your letter requesting my advice. You say that you are seeking love in your life but, as far as I can see, you are already in love – with idleness and sloth. What a lazy fellow you are, unkempt and unwilling to improve. No girlfriend will want to take you on or try to get you to mend your ways.

So, you have a difficult decision to make – will you remain in your dishevelled state and continue with your lazy life or will you improve your personal hygiene and appearance and take the time to find and woo a lovely girl – or 'old doll', as you so unglamorously put it?

I don't like to be brutal, so I hope you won't mind if I do some straight-talking. First of all, your muckers... I beg your pardon, I mean, your *friends*. Are they all like you? Do you think they are suitable company for a young impressionable female dog? Will they be polite in front of her? Are you sure that you are in with a good crowd?

Perhaps you ought to reconsider your choice of friends if you want to introduce them to a new sweetheart.

And secondly, I suggest that you re-examine your motive for wanting a girlfriend. The only reason you give is that you want to make your friends green with envy. If that's the main purpose, then I doubt it is a good foundation for a serious romance and the possibility of puppies. Or does the idea of being a father frighten you? It seems to me you might be one of those guys who is only interested in having a good time, but doesn't want any long-term commitment.

Paddy, it's time for a bit of self-reflection instead of continuing to drift from day to day without any attempt at self-improvement. If, after giving it some thought, you decide you are really serious about finding a girlfriend, then I can put you in touch with my protégé, Maurice, who is setting up a dating agency and we can see if he can help you.

Regards,

Coco

Message from Coco to Karen

14th February 2023

Dear Karen,

Have you noticed the date? Did you remember it is a special day? Yes, it's Valentine's Day – the day when all lovesick puppies can make their feelings known, anonymously, to the object of their desires.

Naturally, I sent a Valentine's card to Milly. It was a really special one with an enormous red satin heart on the front. Inside, it said: 'Roses are red / Violets are blue / I'm golden and handsome / And in love with you.' Do you think she'll guess it's from me? I signed it off: 'Your secret admirer'.

The postie was having a busy day today because he delivered three Valentine cards for me. Of course they were all anonymous, so I've no idea who sent them, but I'm really hoping one of them is from Milly. Perhaps Pippa, my shy little spaniel neighbour, sent another and the third might have been from Precious Petal, because it said, 'I'm silky and fast / A sight to behold / You're friendly and kind

/ With a heart of pure gold.' Isn't that lovely? There's no doubt that my heart belongs to Milly, but it's flattering to know that others may feel a flutter when they think of me.

I hope you got at least one Valentine's card, Karen, but even if you didn't, you know that we puppies all love you to bits.

Love,

Coco x

PS I hope the Gordon Setters didn't send a card to Milly. Even if they did, I bet it wasn't as splendid as mine.

Message from Coco to Karen

22nd February 2023

Dear Karen,

Catastrophe! Calamity! You were absolutely right, I should never have trusted Maurice with the dating agency. He is wreaking havoc.

Not only has he paired up Precious Petal with Spud (she'll be furious with me) and Pippa with Paddy, but he has paired Milly with Knuckles. I'm in a state of panic – everything's in chaos. I shall have to stop his shenanigans and write to Milly straightaway to warn her to have nothing to do with Knuckles. Why, oh why did I not listen to you when you rang alarm bells?

This sorry state of affairs has spoilt the memory of the lovely time I had yesterday – Shrove Tuesday. We had pancakes for tea and I had bacon and maple syrup with mine. Scrummy, scrummy, scrummy. There was some pancake mixture left over, so I was hoping for a bit more of the same this evening, but now I'll have to miss out on that while I sort out this dreadful mess that Maurice has created.

Got to dash.

Love,

Coco x

Message from Coco to Milly

22nd February 2023

Dearest Milly,

Please receive this warning in the spirit in which it is intended – to save you from a scurrilous rogue who has designs upon your innocent and trusting nature. I fear you may be contacted by a reprobate character called Knuckles who will want to woo you, probably with roses and chocolates and that sort of soppy, romantic nonsense. Pay no attention to him, even if he tries to be cute and tells you that his real name is Benjy. Get your housemates to throw him out. He must not be allowed over the threshold and any emails or letters from him should be instantly deleted or thrown in the bin.

    Darling Milly, this is all my fault. As you know, I have been wanting to set up a dating agency for some time and finally, being so busy with my Agony Uncle work for *Pup World*, I delegated it to someone I thought was trustworthy, but who has proved to be completely incompetent. I'm so sorry that your profile was used in the trial. Please, please forgive me. I will make it up to you, I promise.

If Knuckles harasses you, do let me know and I'll get the other boys to sort him out.

Everlasting love,

Coco xxx

Message from Coco to Karen

28th February 2023

Dear Karen,

Whew, I think I've managed to save the day. I've warned Milly, who assures me she is being very vigilant. I also contacted Precious Petal, who says that she's enjoying Spud's company. Apparently he's a scream. She finds him hilarious and is happy to hang out with him so long as it's platonic. He's teaching her puppies how to chase cats. I also had a note from Paddy to say that he's not interested in Pippa because he's met a soulmate called Queenie, a basset hound, and they've become an item. She's fairly mature – he says she's been round the block a few times – and therefore unlikely to be led astray by him. In fact, she seems to enjoy the same kind of lifestyle as he does, so the two of them are perfectly matched. Because no harm has come from Maurice's blunders, I think I'll just have to keep him on a bit longer.

I really do want to make it up to Milly for causing her any alarm, so I need to look my absolute best the next time

I see her. As well as my usual personal grooming, I asked my housemates if I should perhaps start brushing my teeth. They've bought me some liver-flavoured toothpaste, which is really quite tasty, but I don't like the feel of the brush in my mouth. I'll persevere for a bit longer, but I don't know how you humans endure doing it twice a day.

See you in four days' time at the party.

Love,

Coco x

Message from Coco to Karen

4th March 2023

Dear Karen,

I'm so happy and I'm so tired and I'm already snuggled up in my basket, but I just want to write to you before I drop off to sleep to tell you that today has been the best day of my life. The puppies' first birthday party was a great success. It was wonderful to see you and your children again. The cake was delicious and my brothers and sisters are great fun and really friendly. How lucky I am to be part of such a lovely family.

Now that we're one year old, I think you have to stop calling us puppies. We're all grown up and ready to face new adventures and challenges. Thank you so much for all your help and advice during this first year of my life; you've been the best friend I could ever have had.

Lots and lots of love,

Coco x